LIGHTS. CAMERA. MURDER.

THE SILVER SCREEN: Case One

C.S. POE

This is a work of fiction. Names, characters, places, and incidents either are the product of the author's imagination or are used fictitiously, and any resemblance to actual persons, living or dead, business establishments, events, or locales is entirely coincidental.

Lights. Camera. Murder.
Copyright © 2019, 2020 by C.S. Poe

Published by Emporium Press
https://www.cspoe.com
contact@cspoe.com

Cover Art by Reese Dante
Cover content is for illustrative purposes only and any person depicted on the cover is a model.

Published 2020.
First Edition published 2019. Second Edition 2020.
Printed in the United States of America

Digital eBook ISBN: 978-1-952133-18-3
Paperback ISBN: 978-1-952133-44-2

For Reese.
I shine because of you.

INT. PROLOGUE – DAY

GET BENT, DIPSHIT

The love note was scrawled across my grocery list on the refrigerator door. Which was fine. I preferred keeping all my reminders in a central location. Now I knew I needed to pick up milk, sugar, bread, and a new boyfriend.

My cell rang as I splashed some cream into my coffee. I pushed my tortoiseshell glasses up my nose and turned to pick up the phone from the counter behind me.

Caller ID: Nate.

Shocker.

I pressed Accept and put the phone to my ear. "Good morning, sunshine. I got your message."

"You're a sonofabitch, Rory!"

"I've been called worse things by better people."

Nate's audible gasp allowed me enough time to indulge in that first sip of morning coffee. "Only an asshole breaks up over text message," he accused.

I winced at his shrill tone, pulled the phone away from my ear, set it to speaker, and put it back on the countertop. "I only have one rule, Nate."

"Screw your rule."

"And you broke it," I continued without missing a beat.

"Maybe if you were a contributing member in our relationship, I wouldn't have had to find someone else to fuck me senseless."

I stared at the phone and messed my already disheveled hair with one hand. "I told you when we started dating just how much I worked."

"*And?*"

"And if you need it day and night, I'm probably not the most suitable candidate in the dating pool."

Nate let out a frustrated growl and then shouted loud enough to cause mic distortion, "Can you *pretend* like you give a damn right now?"

"It's not worth my energy. You swore to never lie, and I caught you in one." I took another sip of coffee while he sputtered and hissed. "Oh. I'd like my extra key back." I gave the note on the fridge a second glance.

"Burn in hell, Rory."

"Have a good life, Nate."

"Hey, while we're at it—I fucked your coworker too!" he screamed.

"Yeah, I know. Bye-bye." I hit End, promptly deleted Nate's contact information from my phone, and walked out of the kitchen.

LIGHTS. CAMERA. MURDER.

INT. CHAPTER ONE - DAY

The phone was ringing again.

I walked out of the steamy bathroom, wrapping a towel around my waist. I grabbed the cell from the kitchen counter. "Byrne."

"Rory."

I straightened instinctually. "Good morning, ma'am," I said to Violet Shelby, my supervisor at Dupin Private Investigations. She'd been working for the company since the '80s. And while Shelby no longer answered telephones for her boss, but instead *was* the boss, she'd never been able to shake the shoulder pads and power suits of those bygone days.

"It's a morning," she corrected. "What do you know about movies?"

I opened my mouth, paused, then gradually said, "I… took a film-appreciation course in college about a hundred years ago. I mostly recall the insides of my eyelids."

Shelby chuckled. "You talk like you're an old man."

Forty-five, but Shelby hadn't called to ask what year I graduated.

The brisk air of the apartment—a January chill that not even central heating could entirely dissipate—caused gooseflesh to rise on my damp skin.

"Does the name John Anderson mean anything to you?" Shelby asked.

"Wes Anderson's less successful half-brother?"

"Funny," she replied, but her tone implied otherwise. "He's a hotshot television producer here in the city."

Hotshot. That was code for Royal Pain in the Ass.

"Uh-huh."

"I just finished a consultation call with him," she continued. "This will be an undercover case for you."

"As?"

"Well…." There was an uncharacteristically lengthy pause on her end. "It's a little outside the box for Dupin," Shelby warned. "I'm sending you onto a live set. A television show being filmed at Kaufman Astoria Studios out in Queens."

I put a hand on the doorframe and tapped the wall

absently. "What *exactly* is the case, ma'am?"

"Theft. An inside job with a limited timeframe for investigation."

My towel started to slip, and I grabbed one corner, holding it against my hip. "Can you elaborate?"

"Unfortunately not. It'll be up to you to get further details from Anderson. *I know, I know*," she continued, almost as if she sensed my oncoming comment regarding my dislike of intentionally vague details. "But he came to us at the endorsement of *another* hotshot client. You know how they all are. He's looking to have this wrapped up quickly and quietly."

"Aren't they always?"

She snorted. "The suspect will be dealt with internally."

Always sounded a bit mob-ish when Shelby said that.

I started toward the bedroom. "All right. I'm getting ready now."

"I should warn you," Shelby said before I had the opportunity to end the conversation. "There are nearly a hundred people on set. They're all considered suspects."

Dress like a PA.

That was an easy enough instruction—if I knew what the hell a PA was. But Shelby hadn't elaborated on the matter. I suspected she wasn't certain herself and simply reiterated the undercover suggestion provided by Mr. Anderson.

So I googled it.

Physician's assistant.

I kept scrolling on my phone. Google seemed pretty convinced this was what I wanted—even went so far as to suggest courses for becoming a PA, salaries, and stats related to the industry.

I tapped the browser bar and redirected my search to include: what is a film PA?

And there it was at the top of the feed—*production assistant*. Although the title didn't suggest much by way of wardrobe. I stood in the middle of my bedroom, naked but for a pair of boxer briefs, perusing a few blogs on basic film industry etiquette before stumbling upon a recent article that fit the bill: "My First PA Gig. Now What?"

My thoughts exactly.

Not that I was looking to make a career change, but one of the traits of a successful PI was being able to blend into any environment like a chameleon. I'd been Shelby's top undercover man for nearly a decade. I sniffed out business fraud in action like a bloodhound, all while playing the role of some newly hired, clueless stooge. But performing for the benefit of the white-collar crowd around a water cooler was a lot easier than acting in front of *professional actors*. And if I had close to a hundred cast and crew members to sort through regarding this theft of... *something*, I needed to have a firm handle on the sort of environment I was walking into.

The article suggested closed-toed shoes, comfortable layers, and to expect being on my feet all day. All right. So not the correct industry to flaunt four-hundred-dollar, turquoise Fluevog Oxfords. And I definitely wouldn't need to waste time hemming and hawing over a matching tie.

I tossed the phone on the bed.

Gary, my Siamese cat, raised his head from the pillows and made a sleepy pigeon sound in response.

"Sorry, baby," I said, looking over my shoulder. "Daddy's got to work."

Gary yawned and squeaked out another half-hearted *meow*.

"I know," I answered before opening the closet door. "But if you want to keep living this extravagant lifestyle, one of us has to bring home the bread. Right?"

No response.

I glanced at the cat again. He was asleep. Little shit.

I turned my attention back to the closet and sifted through the contents. The clothes were mine, in the sense that I'd paid for them, but I considered my wardrobe that of a theater production's. A costume to suit every situation, every atmosphere, every sort of case a Dupin PI was entrusted with.

For the apparel oft proclaims the man, as Polonius said.

Sometimes, though, dressing for *me* was… a curious predicament. Such occasions were rare, however. I worked a lot. And that was fine. Investigating was what I did—what I *was*. I needn't be concerned with Rory Byrne because my skills were always in demand. Besides cleaning Gary's hairballs off the kitchen floor and being some man's soon-to-be ex-boyfriend, dishonesty was the only consistency in this otherwise topsy-turvy world.

I tugged free a long-sleeve plaid shirt that must have been as old as the grunge movement itself, and a broken-in pair of Levi's from a shelf underneath. I put the clothes on, walked to the bathroom while buttoning the shirt, and took a look in the mirror. I'd definitely grown into my chest and shoulders since the last time I'd worn this homage to Pearl Jam, but it'd do in a pinch. I ran my fingers through my strawberry-blond hair a few times, letting it lie wherever and giving myself a less posh look to match the rest of the ensemble.

I went down the hall, fetched my peacoat from the closet near the front door, and looked back toward the kitchen as I adjusted the jacket collar. Morning sun poured through the blinds onto the table piled with soldering equipment and half-finished projects that were my "de-stress hobby," and cast sharp rays of light across the stainless-steel fridge. Nate's addition to my grocery list shined like a beacon and reinforced my whole point about humans. I returned to the kitchen, gently plucked the note free from under a *Cat Dad* magnet, folded it, and slipped it into my coat pocket.

I didn't like Long Island City.

But I did like their parking fees.

Leaving my car in a garage for the day at a third of the price I'd have paid in Manhattan, I walked four blocks to Kaufman Studios. Despite the bright, sun-shining, blue-sky day, the mercury was flirting with zero. The Queens neighborhood wasn't the wind tunnel that my block on the west end of Midtown tended to be, but the sidewalk still leeched the life out of me with each step, until by the end of my brisk, twelve-minute walk, I felt as if I was walking on pebbles, not toes. I crossed the street and took a right toward the security box outside the studio gates.

"Rory Byrne?"

I stopped midstride and turned, shoulders hunched against the cold.

A short, round man in his fifties was picking his way along the slippery sidewalk. He had a cup of coffee in one hand, a cigarette in the other, wore spectacles too small for his face, and had on a pair of those wraparound earmuffs.

"Yes?" I asked.

He was huffing by the time he reached my side, little plumes of air briefly suspended in the cold. "Tall blond man with glasses, just like Ms. Shelby said. And on time too." He tilted his hand to confirm the hour on his watch and spilled coffee in the process. "Oops—shit."

He hesitated a minute, stuck the cigarette back in his mouth, then offered a free hand. "John Anderson. I'm the client. *Your* client, that is."

"John," I repeated, shaking his hand. "How are you doing?"

"Not good. My nerves have gotten the best of me, I'm afraid," he muttered before removing the cigarette and blowing smoke to one side.

"I see that." I pointed to security. "Would you like to talk inside?"

"No! No, no, we can't do that. Someone might overhear," John hastily answered.

I tucked my hands back into my coat pockets and watched John tap ash from the cigarette almost a bit too aggressively. He shoved the stick into his mouth and chewed on the filter.

"How about you bring me up to speed on this theft."

This was when a client (or ex-boyfriend) decided whether or not they liked me. And it was fine if they didn't. I could still see my investigation through to completion even if they had no interest in a round of beers afterward.

Working on everything from cheating spouses to business fraud to missing persons makes for a lot of potential bullshit to sift through. The best method of approach was to look for deception right out of the gate. I couldn't get caught up in whether John Anderson was a good person.

I actually didn't care.

All I wanted was the truth and nothing more.

"A script was stolen," John said. "*My* script."

"From this television show?"

I studied his jittery movements.

Too much caffeine? Definitely.

Anxiety from being questioned? Probably.

Concealing information? Still uncertain.

"No." John shook his head and removed the cigarette from his mouth. "It has nothing to do with this." He waved his coffee cup at the studios behind me. "*The Bowery*, I mean. It's a script I wrote. Unpublished, but it's still protected by copyright law. This is a theft of my intellectual property. I'm a producer. I know all about—"

I held a hand up.

John frowned, sipped his coffee. "Sorry. I'm a little out of sorts. I haven't slept. I think I've developed an ulcer."

"Can you tell me why you believe the script has been stolen?"

He looked up at me, squinting behind his spectacles. "Because on Saturday night it was in my office, and yesterday it was gone. Are you new at this?"

"Twenty years this June. Who has access to your office besides yourself?"

John blanched a little. "I don't always lock it, if that's what you're asking. It's kind of an honor system, you know?"

What was that saying, the road to hell is paved with good intentions?

"Then who knows about this creative endeavor of yours?"

John shrugged dramatically and huffed a few times. "I haven't the faintest."

A lie.

"I can't do my job if you lie to me, John."

"I really don't know," he insisted. "Honest. I got a little, erm, drunk a few weeks back. I could have talked to anybody." He looked at his mangled cigarette, tossed it to the ground, and stomped on it. John wedged his coffee cup between his chest and arm, fished out a pack of cigarettes from his coat pocket, and lit a new stick. "But I'm here to tell you the script would have been stolen for the *idea*."

"Is this your belief, or do you have proof?"

"B-both," he stammered. "Mr. Byrne—"

"Rory is fine."

John licked his lips. "*Rory.* What do you know about *The Bowery*?"

"Nothing," I said simply.

"It's going to shake the very foundation of the television industry when it premiers," John said. "A historical drama, turn-of-the-century New York City. Thomas O'Sullivan is an Irish gang leader. He's also a gay man in a committed relationship. Throughout the entire show, mind you. None of this tragic, gay-character-dies-in-the-end garbage. And we don't shy away from *anything*. Violence—sure. Sex—of course. But it's the romance that makes this show what it is."

I waited for him to bridge the subject of his stolen script with the plot of this unrelated show being filmed.

Instead, John asked, "You aren't one of those 'I don't mind gay people, but do they have to be gay around me?' folks, are you? Because I'll tell you right now, there will be none—"

"Far from it," I answered calmly.

"Good," he concluded, although he didn't seem to entirely put two and two together on that one. He offered me his coffee cup. "Hold this for me."

I unhurriedly extended a hand, took the Starbucks beverage that weighed in at mostly foamed milk and zero coffee, and watched John remove his pack again. He started to put another stick to his mouth, realized he already had one lit and burning between his lips, and awkwardly put them back in his pocket. He snatched the coffee from my hand.

"My script," John said at length, "is *The Bowery* on steroids. All those things, but bigger. *Better*. We expect—*oh*." He looked up at me. "*Far from it*. You mean you're…."

"My sexuality isn't relevant."

John snorted and then coughed after inhaling wrong. He thumped on his chest a few times and wheezed, "Gay investigator on a gay drama helping a gay producer. It's relevant."

I absently stamped my feet a few times. "You were saying?"

"Er, right. Yes. We expect Emmy nods for *The Bowery*, maybe even an award or two, but my screenplay has more to offer. And the thief *knows* it." John looked up at me again, fire in his beady eyes. "That script was my ticket to getting out of producing. It'd make my career as a writer. Not only in New York, but LA too."

Hotshot, indeed.

"I understand," I answered, keeping my tone neutral. "Tell me why you decided to hire a private investigator instead of reporting this incident to the police."

John's boisterous attitude deflated like a balloon. He took a drag off the cigarette and slammed back the final dregs of his coffee. "I don't want this going to court. I don't want to involve lawyers and unions. I just want to know who's willing to risk their career to claim my idea as their own, so I can squash them like a *bug*."

"You want to blacklist them from the industry?"

John smiled a *wicked* sort of smile. "It's far more satisfying. Besides, we've a lot of high-profile cast and crew on this production. If any of them got wind the police were involved, I could end up with contracts at stake and the thief may escape. And considering the show's content, we can't afford bad publicity before it airs. I mean, for God's sake, we've got Marion Roosevelt playing Tommy." He squinted when I didn't offer an immediate response. "*Marion Roosevelt.*"

"I heard you."

"Do you know who that is?"

"I'm not a connoisseur of television."

"Good grief." John tossed his second cigarette to the ground. "And you call yourself a gay man."

I frowned at that.

He stepped past me and motioned to follow. "Come along, then. Let's get you set up with an ID badge."

INT. CHAPTER TWO - DAY

John wasn't lying. Of this, I was quite certain.

He was stressed. Violated and embarrassed. And angry. He wasn't angry at me, the questioner, but his situation. Listening to the way John had spoken outside, noting the lack of nonverbal indicators that would have had me leaning toward deception, I was convinced he was telling the truth. Where it mattered, at least. He had quite the grandiose ego, but I figured that came with the territory of the industry.

"The beauty of being a PA," John whispered as he led the way down a long hall, "is that it allows you to be *everywhere*." He waved his arms for emphasis. "The office, the set—and no one will be surprised a newbie PA is clueless about the ins and outs of the job." He stopped outside a doorway on the right that opened to a massive staging area with a ceiling nearly twenty feet tall. "We need some kind of cover story, right? Maybe I met you at a film festival, or—"

"No. That's too complex."

"Certainly not."

"Which festival?" I stared John down. "Who was there? What films did you watch?"

He held up both hands. "All right, all right. Point taken."

After a moment of thought, I said, "I'm a family friend looking for a career change. That's all."

John nodded, took a step through the threshold, then turned to me again. "A few suggestions: don't talk back, drink plenty of water, don't sit down, and *never* speak to talent." He walked into the huge room after sharing that tidbit, the *tip-tap* of his shoes bouncing off faraway walls and staged scenery to the right.

"John," I whispered loudly, catching up with him. "You do realize I'm not actually here to work on your show."

"Of course," he muttered, saying hello to passing crew members and not looking at me.

"Then you understand that everyone is a suspect in this theft and I *have* to talk to your cast."

John stopped and looked at me again. "It's not allowed."

"Do you want me to investigate this missing script or not?"

"Of course I do," he hissed, glancing from side to side. "But there are rules on a film set. You don't break them. And the most important is, outside of the director, no one talks to talent. You never know when they might be mentally prepping for a scene—and this show is *heavy* on emotion."

"That's not good enough."

John took off his spectacles and scrubbed his face vigorously with one hand. "Look. If talent approaches *you*, it's okay to chat. But they need to be seen initiating the conversation."

"I'll be sure to face-plant in front of your actors, then," I said dryly.

John patted my upper arm. "Attaboy."

I rolled my eyes to the ceiling once he turned his back.

This investigation was going to be... *a challenge.*

Laughter and radio-edited rap drifted out the open door of some sort of workshop to my left. Immediately ahead of us were two six-foot-long tables packed with an array of juices, coffees, teas, on-the-go breakfast foods, and various high-protein snacks. And at the end of the staging area farther ahead, a massive sliding door opened to the set beyond.

"Art department," John explained, pointing to the left. "And this is crafty. Help yourself when you've got a moment. No one is going to babysit you and make sure you're eating." He led the way onto the dimmed set. "Welcome to *The Bowery*. Specifically, the interior of Thomas O'Sullivan's home."

To my untrained eye, the layout, furniture, even color choices, seemed historically accurate. Definitely rendered as an apartment for someone with a fair amount of money and influence. Nothing out of Millionaire's Row, but also a far cry from some tenement in the Tenderloin District. Perfect for an Irish gangster, I supposed. A few crew members were moving about the area, minutely adjusting props, lights, and calling to each other in lingo sounding reminiscent of military jargon.

"Marion's been featured in *Out* magazine," John was saying, and I looked away from the set design to him. "'Fifty Up and Coming Out Actors.' He was ranked number four, *and* they wrote a snippet about his role as Tommy."

"So he has audience draw?"

"Oh, definitely. He's very charming. The camera loves him. And with this being his first leading role, his net worth is bound to go up a few mil."

Huh.

John touched my arm for a second time and not so discreetly lingered on my bicep. "Come over here." He led the way toward the back right corner of the stage, interrupting a Brooklyn hipster from his work. "Davey, can you spare me a second?"

Davey glanced up from a sheet of paper that looked like a script page, quickly set it aside, and smoothed his beard with one hand while tucking the other under his arm. Even at a foot or two away, I could smell an abundance of earthy, cedar-like cologne trying to mask the smell of too much tobacco. The edges of his fingernails looked discolored. He rolled his own cigarettes. Very edgy, Davey.

"Yes, sir, what can I get you?" he asked John.

"This is Rory Byrne." John brought me into the conversation with a small handwave. "A family friend and our newest PA. Rory, Davey here is Key PA. You'll report to him."

Davey immediately nodded and said, "Sounds good, sir." He still tugged on his beard.

John thanked him, gave me a thumbs-up, and left us.

Davey watched over my shoulder until the producer was suitably out of earshot. "Let me guess—first gig?"

"I'm a quick learner."

"Great," Davey muttered, sounding wholeheartedly unimpressed. Even his beard seemed to object to my presence on set. He grabbed a walkie-talkie from a large bay on a table. "Here you are. Don't forget to do a walkie check. I'm guessing you don't own a surveillance?"

I'd been officially undercover for no more than ten minutes and already found myself someone with a *Star Service* attitude. The man was lucky I wasn't armed. I had at least a decade on this Brooklyn bro, but I was coming to realize that age probably meant little on a film set. Position is where the power was, not in life experience. So I was likely to be getting the college-kid treatment for the remainder of the investigation.

"Figures," Davey said when I hesitated over "surveillance." He grabbed an earpiece similar to those worn by Secret Service. "Put this on and stay out of the way."

I was certain Davey held his dick with four fingers and pissed on three of them.

Nearly one hundred suspects.

Not a workable number. I needed to narrow the scope to a handful of individuals almost immediately.

So the moment Davey sent me to the office to "make myself useful," I asked for a roster of the staff and crew. The production manager met the request with considerable side-eye, but I convinced her of my fledging PA status and talked up wanting to learn crew positions and names.

"You can't keep this," she said, reluctantly handing over a freshly printed sheet. "But go ahead and study it."

I accepted the list. "Thank you, ma'am."

"It's smart of you," she added after a pause. "A good PA should be familiar with all the departments."

I looked up over the rim of my glasses.

"*Including* the office. Most people forget we run the show."

The lines around her face were pronounced, as if

she'd not smiled once in the last… oh… decade. She was stick-thin, with artfully curled brown hair, thick-lensed glasses, and she wore a shade of red lipstick that was particularly aggressive. There was also a touch of hostility in her tone as she spoke.

A bit like, those who can't art, critique art.

Or in this case, those who can't work set jobs oversee from a cozy office chair. I mean, as far as I was aware, the general public was pretty interested in the behind-the-scenes of movie-making, but really, who cared about the phone calls made and emails sent throughout the day that kept the show chugging along?

Interesting.

I had no intention of broaching that bit of reality with—I scanned the list until I found Production Manager, Laura Turner—with Laura. She was especially salty for a Tuesday. And in order to weed out suspects quickly and efficiently, I needed to have key personnel cooperative.

"It's great to meet you, Laura," I said, offering a hand.

She narrowed her eyes skeptically but took my hand in a firm shake. "I don't have any jobs for you. Davey is trying to play a game of volleyball."

And I'm the ball.

"I'm not above stapling and collating," I said by way of suggestion.

"Eager beaver." She opened a few folders on her desk, pawed through some documents, then held up a few loose sheets. "Wow me with your photocopying skills, then we'll discuss stapling."

I accepted the documents, moved around the corner from her desk as Laura indicated, and walked down a short hall. Ahead was the copier, situated between two office doors, one of which read: PRODUCER, JOHN ANDERSON.

A young man, who couldn't have been a day past his twentieth birthday, stood in front of the machine, leaning heavily on the top with both arms. He glanced sideways at me. "It's broken," he explained.

"Ah."

"Have to practically sit on it, or the copy comes out blurry."

Whirr-thck. Whirr-thck. Whirr-thck.

The tray was heavy with tree-pulp sacrifices shooting out at lightning speed, and it didn't look to be finishing up anytime soon.

The man inclined his head awkwardly. "There's another machine down the hall, past the Editing Suite. It's slow as hell, though."

"Thanks for the heads-up." I nodded and moved past him.

I took in my surroundings, memorizing several faces at desks in an open pocket of office space—admin assistants?—and walked by another closed office door, where someone inside was arguing animatedly with what I hoped was a phone on speaker. I came across a massive suite next, darkened and empty through the glass wall, with an impressive computer and digital display setup that *had* to belong to the editing team.

I checked my watch. Just after nine in the morning. And yet, everyone else appeared to have been manning their stations for some time. Did post-production work on a different schedule? I looked at the crew roster I still held on to. There were about a dozen names listed among editing, Foley, and post-audio. Considering John said the script went missing sometime between Saturday and Monday, depending on when these individuals came and went through the office area, it either eliminated them or narrowed my list of suspects to this Dirty Dozen.

I made a mental note to follow up with John about the post-production team in particular, and carried on until I found the lonely photocopier in a darkened, unused wing of the rented out office space. Curious setup. Abandoned desks that'd seen better days were haphazardly strewn around the area. Phones sat in piles on the floor beside wrangled office lines, and there was yet another hall to the left, tarped off for what looked like some minor building maintenance.

I peeled off the Post-it asking for fifty copies, set the papers on the feed, and hit Start. The copier groaned to life. I tugged my surveillance bud free and rubbed at my swollen ear. The tiny nub of plastic was already killing my inner ear, but there was a lot of communication going on between crew members—not that it all translated to plain English—and it was worth the discomfort to hear what was going on.

I slipped the piece back on in time to pick up Davey's

voice saying, "Take it to two."

A second voice confirmed, and their conversation abruptly ended.

Take it to two?

I removed my phone from my back pocket, and as the copier sputtered along, did a quick internet search.

Extend the conversation in private to channel two.

Did this work like John's unlocked-door honor system?

When someone announced they were moving to the next channel, was it simply assumed no one would stick their nose into the chat? Seemed like a good way to hide in plain sight. And if it were this simple to stay in constant communication, it opened the possibility of more than one individual behind the theft.

I took the walkie off my belt and turned the knob on top to the next channel.

"No, sir, but—"

Davey quickly cut the other person off. "You answer to me, kid, *understand?*" he barked in a voice that suggested the only person he could possibly be speaking to in that way was a PA.

"Yes."

"If you go gallivanting off with the art department without reporting to me first—"

"They needed help quick," the PA answered. "I was just trying to lend a hand."

"They're not your boss. I am. And the minute I can't

find your ass at any given second, consider yourself out of a job."

"Yes, sir."

"Report to set."

I twisted the knob back to the main channel and shook my head absently. No suspicious plotting, but for someone who was only one step above the rest of the PAs, Davey had an ego bigger than his beard.

Before leaving the isolated hall, I made a copy of the crew roster, carefully folded it, and tucked it into my sock. I then carried the stack of warm papers, slowing my walk to watch the same young guy still hanging over the finicky copier.

He turned his head, and his expression dropped. "*Jesus*. You finished before me?"

"I only needed fifty." I pointed at the massive stack he was working on. "So are you an administrative assistant or…?"

"I'm a PA," he corrected while leaning harder on top of the copier when one or two of the printouts came out blurry. "Davey sent me here my first day to make copies, and then I wasn't allowed to leave."

"What do you mean?"

He made a face and nodded in Laura's direction. "She won't let me work on set."

"Why's that?" I asked, lowering my voice a bit.

"She's a bitch."

I narrowed my eyes.

He swallowed. "Sorry. I mean—I don't know. Her and Davey don't like each other. One of the other PAs heard from a gaffer who worked on a Disney show with Laura years ago that she'd once been a set PA and got fired."

So there *was* a definite validity to that antagonism toward set jobs I'd picked up from her.

"Anyway," he said as the last page spit onto the tray, "don't make yourself too useful, or she might steal you from set. The office *sucks*."

"Thanks for the heads-up."

I went back to Laura at the front of the office. "Here you are." I handed over the stack of copies and the crew list. "Thanks for letting me look at the roster."

Laura took everything without even a half-hearted thanks. "Go find Davey if you want something else to do."

If there was a test I had to pass in order to be entrusted with her stapler, I guess I'd failed it.

Apparently it was for the best.

I spent my lunch break in the men's bathroom.

"*Shit*." I studied my red, irritated ear in the mirror. I lowered my head, braced my hands on either side of the sink, and took a few deep breaths. Never having to wear that hard nub of plastic again was the biggest incentive I had for closing this case immediately.

"You okay?"

I jerked my head up, and in the mirror's reflection, I saw a man standing in the bathroom doorway. "Oh. Sure." I straightened and turned around.

The stranger was considerably shorter than me, maybe five-foot-five, with a lithe build. He had dark-brown hair, cut and styled in a decidedly outdated fashion, but hell if I could pinpoint the decade in question. He had a beautiful jawline, cheekbones sharp enough to cut glass with, and head-to-toe wore turn-of-the-century clothing.

"You must be one of the show's actors." *Fucking duh*. "Unless suspenders and waistcoats are proper set attire."

He cracked a smile. No teeth, but a cute, boyish smirk crossed his features.

"Grow a beard, and you'd fit right in with Davey at some purposefully divey bar in Williamsburg," I added.

His smile grew at that, and he looked away momentarily, giving his shoes his undivided attention while collecting himself. "I am talent," he agreed.

"A shame."

He brought his gaze up. "How so?"

I shrugged noncommittally. "I was hoping waistcoats were coming back."

"Nothing like a man in a three-piece suit."

"We all have our vices."

My handsome stranger let the door fall shut behind

him as he strolled across the bathroom. "You must be new." He slid his hands into his trouser pockets.

Jesus. He looked so goddamn fine, it was practically criminal.

"What gave it away?" I asked, grinning broadly.

"I don't know your name," he answered.

"You make it a habit to learn everyone's name?"

"I try to."

I reached a hand out. "Rory Byrne."

He removed his hand and accepted the shake. "A pleasure."

"I suspect you have a name as well?"

The stranger flashed that lopsided smile again. "Sure."

I leaned back against the sink, crossed my arms, and gave him another once-over. "You must be… what, about thirty? The most popular name for boys back then was… Michael, I believe."

"I'm thirty-two," he corrected coyly.

"*Oh,*" I said, as if it mattered. "It was still Michael."

He laughed. "I'm afraid my parents used the census records from the 1880s to pick my name, not the 1980s."

"John?"

"Marion," he answered.

"Marion," I repeated, putting two and two together. "*Marion Roosevelt?*"

Shit. Playful conversation with a background

extra was one thing, but the lead actor of the show? Although… he *did* initiate our dialogue, exactly as John had insisted. Keeping a line of communication open with Marion would help me feel out the rest of the cast, as well as crew members above me on the hierarchical ladder.

"Your surprise suggests we had a moment of authentic flirting in the men's bathroom," Marion stated.

"Ah. Yes, but I didn't—"

"Contrary to what the paparazzi would have you believe about film stars, we're just people who sometimes really hope to be treated normally." He leaned forward a bit. "That includes being flirted with."

"I'll remember that."

"Good." Marion moved to the next sink over, turned on the tap, and began washing his hands. "Because you're not half bad at it."

"I've got the beginning part down pat." I turned to watch him. "It's the part that happens *after* where my luck tends to run out."

"That's relatable." He shut off the water and grabbed a paper towel. Marion glanced at me, his brow furrowed a little, and he asked, "So how's your car?"

I instinctively reached up and touched the tender skin. "Agitated."

"Some people have bad reactions to those surveillance pieces," he said, inclining his head at the tube hanging over my shoulder. "Most crew members buy their own."

"I'm still pretty green."

Marion tossed the towel in the trash and stepped closer to examine my ear. He had big, expressive eyes. The actual sort that poets must have in mind when referring to them as windows to the soul. Belatedly, I took in that one eye was a very light green, and the other was actually a dark brown.

Marion must have sensed my staring. "What?"

"Nothing."

"They're real."

"Excuse me?"

"My eyes."

"They're very pretty."

"They're responsible for the contracts," Marion said with a wink. "But luckily, I'm a package deal."

I snorted. "Funny."

"I am sometimes." He took a step back. "I might be able to help with your ear."

"I think I'm a bit too old for kisses on boo-boos."

Marion gave me a direct look, the corner of his mouth upturned again. "In that case… come with me." He walked to the door, opened it, and stepped into the corridor.

I took a breath and followed him out of the bathroom. He led the way down the same hall John had earlier that morning. Toward the end, the left branch led to the production offices. The right went to set. We took the right. Marion walked through the vast staging area, paused long enough at crafty to grab a miniature package of gummy bears, and then brought me through the open set door.

He picked his way around equipment and crew members returning from lunch break. "Paul," he called out to a man seated behind a cart loaded with a plethora of expensive-looking gear, including a multichannel mixing board.

Sound recordist, I determined.

Paul looked up, headphones in his hands, ready to put them on. "Marion. What's up?"

"Do you have any extra earpieces?" Marion asked, tearing open the candy package. "The molded ones."

"Looking to become my apprentice?"

Marion smiled, but it was a different smile than what I'd experienced in the bathroom. Instinctual. Polite. A bit reserved, even. "My friend here is having issues with the cheapo ones they give PAs."

Paul only acknowledged my existence when Marion motioned to me with one hand. He leaned back in his chair and stared at the side of my head. "He sure is. You're what—about a medium?"

"Large where it counts," I joked, because I honestly had no idea what he was referring to. I glanced sideways at Marion.

He'd crossed one arm over his midsection and placed a hand against his mouth, failing to hide his amusement.

Nice to know my childish comment hadn't worked

against me.

"Yeah, I bet," Paul said sardonically. He pushed his chair back, leaned down, and retrieved a leather pouch from the bottom shelf of the cart. He unzipped it, sifted through various oddities I'd never seen outside of the personal-care aisle in Duane Reade, then offered a pink earpiece still in its packaging. "Don't lose it. And you owe me twenty bucks."

"Thank you," I said graciously. "I really appreciate it." I tore it open, stuck the piece onto the end of the plastic tube, and fit it in my ear.

"Better?" Marion asked me as he stepped away from Paul.

I nodded, following him. "A lot better. How'd you know about these?"

"I try to be conscious of the crew."

I raised an eyebrow.

Marion simply shrugged. He popped a red bear into his mouth.

I started to speak, but someone called Marion's name from behind, interrupting the last chance I had to… well, do *what*, exactly? Flirt some more? Marion was undoubtably gorgeous, devastatingly sweet, and I was reluctantly enamored at first sight. But showing interest in a guy while working a case—where said heartthrob had not been ruled out as a suspect—was strictly against the policies of Dupin Private Investigations. I was merely rebounding after severing ties with Nate that morning.

And rebounds were fine.

Just not with Marion Roosevelt.

Nothing to see here. Move along, Rory.

A man easily my height and build, with black hair and a matching goatee peppered with silver, came toward us. He wrapped a large hand around Marion's arm and tugged him sideways. "I need to speak with you."

Marion's physical response would have likely gone unnoticed if I wasn't trained to read body language. The muscle to the right of Marion's mouth, which gave him such a pleasing, crooked smile, tightened. His heterochromatic eyes narrowed at the same moment. Maybe it was an over-the-top and unprofessional description, but the light in Marion's face seemed to fade.

"Yes, of course," Marion answered, flashing a fake smile worthy of an Oscar. He followed Mr. Top-Ten-Beards-in-Hollywood-According-to-BuzzFeed toward the set without so much as a second glance my way.

EXT. CHAPTER THREE - NIGHT

"So?" John asked impatiently.

We stood on the sidewalk outside the studios after dark. It was bitterly cold, and I pulled the collar of my coat up on the back of my neck before stuffing my hands deep into the pockets. Most of the crew had clocked out for the evening, giving John the opportunity to circle back with me for the first time since that morning to harass me for details I didn't have.

"Who did it? Who stole it?"

"John, please," I interrupted. "It's not that easy. These situations can take some time."

"I don't have time," he protested. "Once this show wraps on principal photography, that's it. The thief gets away. *Forever!*"

"I'd like you to clarify a few details for me," I said,

reeling him back from the ledge he was about to fling himself from. "Tell me about the post-production team."

"What about them?"

"While I did some work in the office, I noticed their suite was empty."

"Yes. They arrive later in the day—after lunch. The schedule allows them to finish work from the previous day, and then by the time Ethan and I are done on set, we can sit with the editors and go over dailies and watch some rough cuts."

"And Ethan's the director, is that right?" I'd gathered that much after a sneak peek at the crew roster when work resumed after lunch and Mr. Goatee was the one calling *action!*

"Ethan Lefkowitz," John said with a nod.

I grunted. "And on Sunday, was the editing team working?"

"No. None of us were. Double time on Sunday. We avoid it at all costs."

"And you are *absolutely* certain your script was in the office Friday and Saturday, but gone by Monday?" I pressed.

"Yes, and I'll tell you—we had a pick-up scene to shoot Saturday. A character that only appears in one episode had a scheduling conflict. We *had* to shoot Saturday. So I was here. I went to my office afterward, did some minor editing on the script, but I was so tired, I didn't stay late."

"But production had for sure wrapped by then?" I asked, using the term I'd heard the assistant director call out earlier on set to indicate our job was done for the day.

John nodded vigorously. "*And* we had no post-production crew on Saturday."

"What about the office staff?"

"I recall a few," he confirmed.

I ran my fingertips through my hair a few times. "What about the possibility of someone coming in to work on an unscheduled—"

John shook his head dramatically. "No, no, no. Union rules, Rory. That doesn't happen without the assistant director or production coordinator knowing. News would travel like a wildfire in California."

"Fine. Tell me what time you arrived yesterday morning."

"Seven."

"And the script was already gone?"

"I, er—" John hesitated. He started patting his jacket, searching for his cigarettes, no doubt. "I'm not certain. *Probably.* But I didn't take notice until I'd gone back to my desk around ten to make a phone call."

Based on this timeline—unreliable though it was—I could rule out the entire post-production team simply because they hadn't been in the building over the weekend, nor did they arrive on Monday early enough to abscond with the script. I couldn't clear all those admins in the bullpen, though. Either before John's early arrival yesterday, or in between his back-and-forth to the set, any one of those staffers could have been presented the opportunity to slip inside his room nestled between the production manager around the corner and show accountant in the next office over.

I also couldn't rule out Ethan Lefkowitz, the director. It seemed ridiculous that a director would have a reason or desire to steal a script. As far as my understanding went, he was near the top of the food chain on a film set. He held a lot of power over the content, gained prestige for overseeing the performances, and was likely being compensated quite well. On the other hand, if there was a crew member John would have casually spoken to about his personal writing, or mentioned it to in a moment of bragging, it'd be someone he considered his equal.

Plus, I hadn't been able to silence the warning bells in my head after witnessing the domineering way Ethan touched Marion, and said actor's *almost* flawless performance to cover his discomfort.

Something was wrong there.

Something that merited further inquiry.

So where'd that leave me? Twelve suspects down, only about eighty to go?

"I'd like a list of all the cast members who worked Friday, Saturday, and Monday," I said.

"Sure." John tugged a cigarette free from a crushed pack and lit it. He stuck the stick in his mouth and then immediately took it out when the request sank in. "You think the thief is talent?"

"I think nothing. I want the names in order to do cross-referencing."

John's face was pinched, his spectacles lifting up with the movement of his muscles. He took a few puffs, then whipped out his phone. "What's your email?"

I recited my Dupin address, retrieved my cell from a pocket, and less than a minute later it dinged with an incoming email. I swiped, opened the message, and several PDFs with the cast schedule loaded. "Great," I murmured, studying the times and names.

Marion Roosevelt.

Marion Roosevelt.

Marion Roosevelt.

So there was no crossing my—*their*—heterochromatic actor off the suspect list yet.

"Does Mr. Roosevelt work every day?" I asked.

John turned his head and blew smoke into the darkness. "Most. Marion is a true gem. No complaints, no egotistical, star-studded temper tantrums, and he doesn't use a stand-in."

I turned off the phone's screen and stared at John.

He shook his head like, *Oh, right, this man has no idea what I'm talking about.* "Some actors have a double stand in for them when shooting the lines and reactions of the other talent. Marion is vehemently against that. He'll be on set twelve, sometimes fifteen hours just to respect the process of his fellow actors."

"He seems like a decent person," I agreed.

"To say the least." John tapped the end of his cigarette. "Do your cross-referencing-what-have-yous with those names, but Marion is *not* a suspect. In fact, I'm asking you as the client, don't investigate him."

"John, that's not how—"

"I can hire someone else," John threatened.

That'd piss off Shelby.

"No one is above suspicion."

"If I lose Marion, the whole show falls apart. There's no appeal without him. No audience draw. The man is just *this side* of perfect," John babbled.

Picture perfect.

"He's not a thief," John continued. "If there's one person I'm certain is innocent, it's Marion. So I'm telling you, I do not want him investigated."

I took a deep breath and let the air briefly freeze my lungs. After a slow release, I avoided a response by motioning to the pack John still held in one hand, and asked, "Can I bum one of those?"

He looked surprised but offered a cigarette. "You shouldn't smoke."

"Yeah," I agreed, accepting his lighter next and setting the flame to the tip. "How much is your script worth?"

John wiped his forehead with the sleeve of his coat. "It's a *really* good idea," he said by way of answering.

"If the thief isn't caught now," I continued, before taking a brief drag, "you could still easily prove the project is yours."

"True. It's not like I don't have copies. But if *I* stole it, I'd rework it, you know?"

"Hmm."

"Harder to prove it's stolen when it's not outright plagiarism," John murmured, looking at the ground. "But the idea would be tainted after that." He sounded almost... *melancholy*.

"Do you know of anyone on set having issues? Finances, things like that?" I tried.

"I'm not their damn mother."

I raised an eyebrow.

"Sorry," John said quickly. "Oh boy. Too much nicotine." He flicked the cigarette. "Not enough sleep."

I checked my watch. "Why don't you go home? I'll see you tomorrow?"

"Tomorrow," John echoed, but he headed back in the direction of the studio.

I turned to Thirty-Fifth Avenue and walked toward the end of the block. Potted plants lining the Kaufman entrance were buried in freshly fallen snow, and my shoes crunched loudly on the salted sidewalk.

"Rory Byrne, are you following me?"

I looked over my shoulder while taking another drag from the cigarette. Marion emerged from the darkness, as if he'd detached from the night itself and taken human form. "I think you're following me," I countered.

I caught his smile as he walked under a lamppost before coming to a stop beside me on the street corner. "Think I can steal one of those?" he asked, pointing discreetly at the cigarette hanging between my lips.

I removed it and said, "I actually bummed this one." I twisted my hand around and offered the filtered end.

"Are you sure?" Marion asked.

I nodded. "It's a bad habit."

"Don't I know it," he said before accepting. "I've been trying to quit. One of those New Year's resolutions."

"Not working out?"

"January came in like a freight train," he said with a melodic chuckle and careless wave of his hand.

I allowed myself a brief, unabashed moment to study Marion. The way the orange glow of the nearby tungsten bulb cut sharp shadows across his face. The way his cheeks hollowed a little when he inhaled. The way he licked his bottom lip after blowing smoke.

"What?" he asked. Marion's voice was deep, but he didn't speak with the strength of his diaphragm. So his tone was lighter, gentler.

A careful and practiced sort of speech.

"May I ask you a question?"

"Okay." He smiled. Like he knew what was coming—was expecting it.

So I threw him a curveball. "Do you enjoy working with Mr. Lefkowitz?"

Marion's facial expressions flickered like an old television. Charm gave way to confusion, to disappointment. Then he squared his shoulders, cleared his throat, and inhaled another breath of smoke. "Why do you ask?"

I shook my head a little.

A black car pulled up to the curb. The driver got out, called a greeting to Marion, and walked around the trunk to the back passenger door. He opened it and waited.

Marion held out the cigarette. "Thank you for the nicotine."

I accepted the stick. "Sure."

"That's my ride."

"I figured."

Marion looked up at me, considered something to himself, but ultimately said, "Have a good night."

"You too." My cell rang as I watched him walk to the hired car. I reached into my pocket, took out my phone again, and looked at the screen. It was the Big Boss.

"Rory," Marion called.

I glanced up, thumb hovering over the Accept button.

"If you're around tomorrow," he started, blunt fingertips tapping the top of the car door in a hesitant manner. "After lunch—I'll be washing my hands again."

Hell. What a bad week to end it with Nate. I felt stripped and naked. Defenseless against the subtle charms of an unconventionally handsome man who absolutely *knew* I was goddamn smitten.

No.

Do not pass go.

Do not collect two hundred dollars.

I smiled apologetically and did the only thing I could to break the moment. I answered the call. "Byrne."

"Rory. Have a moment?"

"Yes, ma'am." I kept my gaze on Marion as he climbed into the car, shut the door, and the vehicle sped off into the night. I flicked my cigarette, crossed the street, and went in the opposite direction, toward the parking garage.

"How's TV life?"

"About as hectic and ego-driven as you'd expect it to be."

Shelby's laugh was warm. "So I won't be losing you to the limelight?"

"Afraid not, ma'am."

"Good."

"The theft was of a script. An unpublished piece Anderson wrote. It was taken from his office," I explained without prompting.

"I see. Were you able to narrow the scope of the investigation from that ridiculous initial suspect count?"

"A bit," I said, switching the phone to my other side and putting my cold hand in my pocket. "The post-production department can be omitted on account of their scheduling. But there's still a lot of coming and going to take into consideration. Some crew members, electricians and such, are more restricted in duties, I've noticed. I'm fairly confident in disregarding them as suspects on the grounds that there's little if no way for them to step into the production office without it being questioned."

"But?" she prompted.

"But there is a pecking order on film sets unlike anything I've seen before. From a sociological standpoint, it's fascinating. From an investigative one, it's extremely frustrating."

Shelby made a humming sound. Her thinking-out-loud noise.

I continued. "On the one hand, it narrows the scope considerably, as the only individuals who have immediate access to John are those in positions of power themselves. But not all these department heads have an obvious motive. There are some low-ranking crew members I'm having to consider as well."

"How would they know about the script if they don't speak with the producer like you say?" Shelby questioned.

"Besides the fact that Anderson can't remember who he may have spoken to about it?" I said with a *touch* of annoyance. "Everyone on set has a walkie." I dug out my parking receipt as I reached the garage.

An attendant stepped out of a booth, took the paper from my outstretched hand, and went to fetch my car.

"There's a process for having a private discussion, but everyone has access to the channel in question. It's possible any number of conversations could have been overheard and used to an individual's advantage."

"What do you think about Anderson?" Shelby asked at length. "Is this script of his worth a lot?"

"It may be worth nothing."

"Oh?" I could hear the wry smile in that single word.

I glanced toward the ramp leading from the underground garage as my car's headlights lit up the street. "I've noticed a considerable amount of hostility and abuse of power among certain individuals. I don't believe the script itself is worth money. It's the idea. And if the idea *is* a moneymaker, it could be a reasonable assumption that someone was willing to steal it in order to get out from under someone else's thumb."

Gary was sitting on the table when I entered the apartment. My soldering iron was dangling over the edge by its cable, the floor was littered with strips of PVC shrink tube, a partially unspun roll of alloy wire for soldering, and a pair of wire strippers were under a chair. He meowed loudly as I shut the door and hung up my coat.

"Hi, baby." I walked toward him, leaned over, and kissed his head. "Is this some sort of social protest?"

I bent to collect the fallen hobby items, and the cat jumped onto my shoulders. He meowed a second time before digging his claws into my shirt and holding on as I straightened and set everything on the tabletop. I scratched Gary's chin while I walked into the kitchen. I didn't bother with the light. I grabbed a beer from the fridge, then went to the couch on the other side of the room from the table and sat down. The cat climbed onto my chest, butt directly in my face before he turned, got comfortable on my lap, and continued to voice his disapproval over my tardiness.

"Sounds like you had a rough afternoon." I leaned over awkwardly, pulled free the crew roster from where it'd been wedged in my sock all day, and tossed it onto the cushion beside me. I untwisted the top from the beer bottle and took a sip. "Did you want to hear about my—no? Okay. Keep going."

Gary talked while I kicked off my sneakers, grabbed the remote from the coffee table, turned on the television, and took another drink. He was still vocalizing as I went into the TV guide and did a search of programs by actor.

M A R I O....

Marion Roosevelt popped up as a suggested name, and I tapped Search. One movie was available for immediate viewing. *Bastard Boyfriend*. A new release too, although I considered anything post *Star Trek: The Next Generation* to be a relatively new release. Film-related entertainment had simply never held my interest or imagination. And once I'd finished college and was hired with Dupin, every minute of my life had been dedicated to my profession.

Followed by Gary.

And then men.

In that order. That's how I liked it. Zero drama, maximum efficiency.

I hit Play on *Bastard Boyfriend.*

I found Marion to be extremely attractive. I wouldn't have bothered watching his movie if I didn't enjoy staring. Physically, he was everything I liked in a man—slender, toned, shorter than me, and pretty in a decidedly masculine way. He wore a suit like it'd be a sin to undress him. And those eyes. Thirty seconds into this movie and Marion already conveyed more emotion with those heterochromatic eyes than his costars did with their lines.

But he didn't get a free pass in this investigation simply because his ass looked fine in tweed.

And that was all there was to it.

Gary meowed loudly in my face, crossed blue eyes giving me a level look.

"Sorry." I continued petting him, and his eyes fluttered shut in contentment.

I leaned over once again, set my beer on the coffee table, picked up a pen, then snatched the crew roster. I unfolded the printout and diligently crossed off each post-production name. I wrote Marion's name in the margin, crossed it out, then wrote it again. Outwardly, there seemed very little reason for him to betray John and bite the hand feeding him. He'd landed what sounded like a dream job for most actors, and his millions were expected to continue multiplying. Marion's motive may have been more unconventional, of course, although my gut was saying no. But I wasn't paid for instinct. I was paid to produce facts and hard evidence.

For certain, there were a few folks raising red flags that I needed to do a background check on and shadow tomorrow. Some of the key personnel on *The Bowery* represented a number of humanity's greatest sins to such a *T*, Dante himself couldn't have done better.

Envy—Production Manager, Laura Turner.

Wrath—Director, Ethan Lefkowitz.

Pride—Key PA and my good pal, Davey.

INT. CHAPTER FOUR - DAY

My reports on the three musketeers came back surprisingly bland the next morning. No criminal records, no serious debt beyond an unruly credit card, consistent employment for the last five years. There was nothing to suggest financial constraints were a factor in the theft, if indeed Laura, Ethan, or Davey were guilty beyond being Grade A assholes with excellent credit scores.

But I wasn't able to easily shake off their abrasive personalities and consider them clean like post-production. A major factor in this case was the environment itself. This wasn't some high-rise office in Midtown caught performing underhanded accounting, because in that setting, it was *always* about the money. Ego, popularity, and fame came with the territory of the film industry. And if a crime was committed in order to rise in the ranks of power, well, there wasn't any sort of background check I could run on that.

I was further cockblocked that morning by Davey's unrelenting attitude toward me. I was certain he didn't suspect I was anything but an inexperienced PA, but that didn't stop him from taking every afforded opportunity to kick me off set in order to complete some menial task for another department. I understood that PAs were, by their very nature, assistants to any part of production, but it seemed counterproductive to send them away from the very location where they needed hands-on experience the most.

Or in my case, where I needed to be in order to oversee Davey's movements. Specifically because his job *also* allowed for a great deal of flexibility, and I wanted to confirm for myself *exactly* what he did with his time on and off set. I'd noticed, upon arriving at the same time as the crew, that there were several set PAs who answered to Davey. And like me, he sent them elsewhere.

Why?

Less eyes on his movements?

If it were only me being punted about, I'd say it was because he resented the way in which John had dropped me into his lap yesterday. But all of us?

"The only job lower than a PA is an intern," said the wardrobe assistant.

I'd been sent upstairs, where the costume department

stored all their clothing, to aid Elizabeth Something-or-Other, who could have been Bettie Page's contemporary sister, in a "double-check" of all the attires organized by episode and character.

"Some people in the industry get shit on when they first enter," she continued while reading the labels on hanging garments and cross-checking each with her clipboard. "So once they get to a position of power, they return the favor and claim newbies gotta earn their keep like they did." She stared at me over the rack. "Davey's swell. *If* he likes you. If not, I hear you end up making photocopies all day for Laura."

"I did that yesterday."

She shook her head, took a hanger, and moved it to a different rack. "Want a piece of unsolicited advice?"

"Sure."

Elizabeth paused and looked at me again. "Make yourself useful to someone other than Davey. But be subtle. No one likes a know-it-all PA. If you can be That Guy, though, departments will request you by name. Davey won't be in a position to say no to someone over his head."

"Won't that piss him off?"

"You want to get a call back for a job in the future or not?"

"Point taken."

Elizabeth nodded and returned her attention to the clipboard. "Do you have Tommy O'Sullivan's episode three suit on that side? Gray tweed."

I looked down at the line of clothes in front of me and quickly pawed through them. "Right here." I removed Marion's costume and passed it to her.

Elizabeth muttered something about interns under her breath as she relocated the outfit.

"So how do you suggest I make friends with the crew?" I gently prodded.

"You have any gum?"

I frowned and patted my jeans pockets. "I have Altoids." I held up a miniature tin of breath mints.

"That'll work. Everyone wants fresh breath after lunch."

"Ah. Bribery." I laughed a little.

"Davey for Rory," said the static voice in my earpiece.

I reached for the mic button of the surveillance. "This is—er—go for Rory."

Goddamn set talk.

"What's your 20?"

I resisted rolling my eyes. As if he didn't already know where I was. "I'm still upstairs in wardrobe storage."

"Report to set."

"All right."

"*Copy,*" Elizabeth whispered loudly. "Say you copy."

"Copy," I hastily added into the mic. "Thanks," I told her before stepping out of the maze of clothes. "I've got to run."

"Hope it's not for coffee," she called after me, tone sympathetic.

I left the stuffy storage room, hurried down the back staircase, and ran along a practically hidden hallway lined with dressing rooms. I stopped at the side entrance to the stage. The red light, which indicated recording-in-session, was off, and the door had been propped open. I stepped inside. Crew was busily adjusting set pieces and relocating the camera when I heard Davey shout my name.

I turned to my left, wove around equipment, and found him standing beside Paul, the sound recordist who'd provided me with the new earpiece yesterday.

"We need you to make a run," Davey stated.

"Where to?"

Paul, still sitting, dropped a frayed cable into my hand. "An audio rental house a few blocks from here. Camera ripped my timecode cable, and there isn't time for me to make one."

I held up either end, studied the connectors, and realized the perfect opportunity to get in with a different department had just presented itself to me. This case could be wrapped more quickly than anticipated if I could hang out around Paul. I'd have a vantage point from which to study the interactions of Ethan, Davey, and—whether or not John liked it—the talent. "If you have the supplies," I began, looking back at him, "I can make this for you right now."

"We'll buy one," Davey quickly interjected.

Paul held up a hand at Davey. "These cables are like eighty bucks, cowboy. I don't want to get in a tiff with Laura." He gave me a concentrated stare. "You know how to solder? Because LEMO connectors aren't a joke."

"I'm certified. Give me the schematics, and I can do it in fifteen minutes."

Paul made a gruff sound under his breath. He tore a piece of paper from a small notebook, hastily drew a wiring diagram, and held it out. "Make sense?"

"Yes."

"Good." He stood, went to a hard-shell case covered in logo stickers propped up against the back wall, then returned a moment later with a Ziploc bag full of unassembled connector parts and lengths of cable. "There's a soldering iron in the art workshop."

I was back in sixteen minutes, but I did have to allow the soldering iron to heat first, so the discrepancy seemed a reasonable excuse. And the cable worked, much to my relief, Paul's gratitude, and Davey's annoyance—so all was right with the world.

"Take a listen," Paul said, handing me his big headphones. "What do you hear?"

After proving myself useful, Paul kept me at his side and dismissed Davey, like I'd hoped. And hell, unlike most of the crew, he was more than happy to talk about the ins and outs of his job. Should I have actually been a PA, Paul would have been the saving grace of my career thus far.

But I wasn't a PA. I was a PI.

Big difference.

So every little detail he taught me about mics or timecode or whatnot was simply one more opportunity to glean information regarding his interactions with individuals on set. It gave me a chance to present myself as someone he could trust. Someone to complain to. To confide in.

I put the headphones on my ears, and after a moment, said, "Sounds like clothes rustling."

"That's right. It's Marion's tie mic. No one notices good sound until it's bad."

I set the headphones down and looked toward the set. Marion was standing in the middle of the scene, arms crossed, shifting absently from foot to foot as someone from makeup touched up his face. Ethan was talking animatedly with a second actor who, I think, portrayed Tommy's lover in the show. John sat in one of those folding director's chairs several feet away, texting a mile a minute and seemingly oblivious to the nonsense Ethan was spouting.

The assistant director yelled a warning that camera was almost ready to roll on the new angle.

Paul stood and motioned for me to follow. The set was bright and uncomfortably warm under the thousands of watts of light, but I guess it was something one simply got accustomed to. Marion lowered his hands to his sides as Paul replaced the woman who'd been brushing his jawline. He silently lifted his chin when Paul indicated what he meant to do. The sound recordist hastily loosened the knot on Marion's tie and deftly adjusted a hidden microphone in the clothing.

Marion must have seen me. It would be impossible to miss my towering presence directly behind Paul. But his gaze was focused on some distant point over my shoulder. His expression was hard. *Dangerous*. So unlike the sweet man with the boyish charm from yesterday. It'd taken a moment for it to sink in that Marion was on the clock. This was his work. Not only was he an actor, and quite a good one if *Bastard Boyfriend* was anything to go by, but in *The Bowery*, he portrayed a high-class, violent criminal. He must have been in some… dark character zone.

The second actor detached himself from Ethan at that point, stepped behind Marion, put a hand on his shoulder, and whispered, "That entire tirade can be summed up as: be more sad."

Still staring at that faraway point, Marion made a quiet shushing sound under his breath.

"I'm sick of it," the other actor continued. "Was I hired to parrot back Ethan's bullshit acting or do the role myself?"

"All set," Paul declared, taking a step away from Marion. "Let's go," he said to me as he moved out of the glow of lights and headed for his sound cart.

I heard Marion say, "Do the scene as we discussed. I'll handle Ethan."

I dared one glimpse over my shoulder. Marion put a hand on his costar's chest, gave him an affirming little pat, and walked out of the scenery and surrounding props.

"Out of the shot, PA," someone near camera shouted.

I hauled ass back to the mess of sound equipment.

"Always take a listen after making a mic adjustment," Paul said without skipping a beat, as if we'd been talking the entire time. He handed me his headphones again before busying himself with buttons and levels on his mixing board.

Not that this multimillion-dollar production should be trusting *my* untrained ears, but I obediently put the headphones on and took a listen. I heard nothing but the set ambience—faraway voices, the sound of equipment and tools—then Marion's sudden voice gave me a start.

"I think James did wonderful during rehearsal."

"*You* think?"

I raised my head, scanned the massive room, and found Marion in a secluded corner, speaking with Ethan.

"Yes," Marion said, quiet but insistent. "And telling him *how* to do this scene instead of helping him find it—"

"He's not finding shit, Marion," Ethan spat, voice farther away but still heard through the tie mic. "I was hired to make this show a triumph, and James is an albatross."

"Ethan."

I picked up a fluttering, almost thumping reverberation from Marion's microphone. Quick but constant.

Like—a heartbeat.

Marion's heart was pounding so hard, the microphone was actually picking up the sound.

"Are you the goddamn director?" Ethan retorted.

"No," Marion whispered, the courage in his tone waning considerably. As if this was a battle he knew from the start he'd lose.

Even from where I stood, I could see Ethan step closer and point a finger in Marion's face that in turn caused Marion to visibly bend away from the invasion.

"Remember who made you."

"We are *not* a package deal," Marion replied.

"We'll see about that," Ethan answered. "Get back to one."

I didn't like Ethan.

Although the reason I detested the man was admittedly a bit unrelated to the actual reason for my being at Kaufman Studios. I'd had hours on set in which to study him, and Ethan's treatment of the talent was subtle but reprehensible. With John however, he was completely cooperative, communicative, and polite. I could imagine their rapport flourishing into something collaborative—like maybe directing John's script. Ethan had moments with him that seemed a bit too… ass-kissy, but it was clear he knew not to shit where he ate. And either John enjoyed the attention, or didn't notice he was being sucked up to. The producer's slightly oblivious personality made me think the latter.

John had already established that he and the director left set together in the evenings in order to watch edits in the office. So despite Ethan's behavior suggesting he'd never double-cross John, the fact that he'd been in the vicinity of the script countless times couldn't be disregarded. However, it was worth noting that Ethan hadn't once left set during production hours. So while I had no hard evidence that proved him highly suspect *or* innocent, should Ethan had been the one to steal the script, it likely would have been in the evening.

There'd been no editing done over the weekend. And John said his script was still safe in his office Saturday night.

But still. Ethan was an egotistical prick to the nth degree.

He wasn't a director.

He wasn't even an *artiste*.

He was a manipulator and a bully.

I needed to speak with John to clarify what time Ethan had arrived on set Monday morning. But I also needed to bring his treatment of talent to John's attention. If he was so protective of Marion and of keeping him on *The Bowery*, John needed to be aware of the fact that actors were uncomfortable on set with the one man allowed to interact with them.

Upset and frustrated, even.

I simply couldn't in good conscience look the other way when Marion visibly recoiled around Ethan Lefkowitz. No success was worth it—not my case, and not a groundbreaking television show—if it came at the expense of another's emotional safety.

I rose from the lunch table as that revelation reared its ugly head. I was willing to compromise—*no*. It wasn't compromising anything if I simply asked John to be more cognizant. I moved with the intention of making a quick dash to his office, when a few seats down, Davey stood as well. I watched him pick up his jacket from the back of the chair, pull his arms through the sleeves, pat the pockets, and walk out of the room.

Cigarette break.

Shit.

Davey had been doing a good job at keeping real low-key that day. Even being granted set access all morning, I'd found it difficult to keep eyes on him and had been unable to confirm where he occasionally disappeared to. Now that I had a hot second in which to corner him, I wanted to go the opposite direction and spend the last few minutes of my break with John. I hesitated on my feet, mentally flip-flopping over which angle was more important. I'd even reacquainted myself with nicotine last night, after years of being smoke-free, because of the tobacco stains I'd noticed on Davey's fingernails. A cigarette break was the closest thing to water-cooler chitchat with these folks, and I couldn't afford to miss those opportunities.

After all, people love to talk.

People love to *gossip*.

It didn't matter if it was a high-rise, corporate accounting office, or the back lot of a film set. Universally, humans craved knowledge of one another. Gossip was a tool—a currency—in which individuals bonded or excluded those who didn't support a group mentality. Statistically speaking, Davey would spill something interesting to me sooner or later. There was no denying human hardwiring. Also, taking into consideration his antipathy toward me, it would likely result in boasting to belittle me. And that was fine. Because when men *shoot the breeze*, it's usually in regard to status or position.

In other words, a perfect cocktail for an admission of guilt without their knowledge.

"How's the weather up there?" a woman beside me asked, looking up. "Breezy?"

I laughed politely. Automatically "I'd love to have a quick smoke. Where should I go for that?"

She pointed in the direction Davey slipped out. "Take the elevator to the ground floor, but then go out the door on your immediate left. It's the loading dock. Everyone smokes back there."

"Thanks."

She finger-gunned me and continued eating lunch.

I grabbed my peacoat and put it on while walking out of the room and down the long hall. I buttoned the front before slowing outside the bathroom door where I'd met Marion.

I almost stopped.

Almost poked my head inside.

"After lunch—I'll be washing my hands again."

The rebound of a lifetime. But I had a job to do.

I reached the elevator and pressed the button with my thumb. The doors opened with a *ping*, I stepped inside, chose the first floor, and rode it down. The ground-floor hallways were decorated with framed movie and television posters of productions filmed at the studios—*Sesame Street*, *Nurse Jackie*, *Orange is the New Black*. Granted, I was only familiar with the big yellow bird….

I went out the door marked LOADING DOCK and feigned surprise when Davey turned at the intrusion. "Sorry. Ah, do you mind if I smoke out here too?"

Davey raised his cigarette, licked the paper, and carefully rolled it shut. "I don't own the place." He put it in his mouth, fetched a Zippo lighter from his pocket, and lit the end.

I took a few cautious steps forward, the door falling shut behind me. I tapped a cigarette out of a pack I'd bought that morning, turned away from the wind, and lit it. I took a few drags and watched as Davey ignored me in favor of scrolling through a Facebook feed on his phone. "How long have you been in the industry?" I asked at length.

"Five years," he replied absently.

"Wow."

He grunted.

"Did you go to school for film?"

He laughed at that and looked up. "I earned my career by getting on set and *doing the job*." He started to put the cigarette to his mouth before pausing long enough to say, "And a family friend didn't help."

Oh, touché, you little dick.

I shrugged and leaned out the open dock to tap ash onto the pavement below. "John's a decent guy." I gauged how much of Davey's cigarette was left and took a deep drag from mine. The rush of nicotine made my head swim. "The PA gig is tough," I said after blowing the smoke into the biting-cold afternoon air.

Davey finally smiled, wide and sharkish. "Giving up already?"

"No, no. But I don't think I could make it my career."

"It's a stepping-stone," Davey answered, his tone inflecting upward in a curious, knee-jerk response to some perceived criticism in my comment. He reached up and combed his fingers through his Gimli beard.

I kept my face neutral but carefully prodded at that exposed insecurity. "What's that?"

"No one wants to be a PA until the job cripples them."

"I see."

"I've got a way out, in fact," Davey continued. He nodded to himself, took a final drag, then squashed the leftover bit of cigarette into an overflowing ashtray some other previous crew member had left behind. "I recently took on a project. Working on lining up investors too. I won't be organizing lemmings for a paycheck forever."

I smiled and licked my lower lip.

INT. CHAPTER FIVE - NIGHT

John was walking toward the elevator. Another day of production had wrapped on *The Bowery*. I'd just stepped out of staging and into the long corridor when I recognized the shorter man from the back, dressed for going outside.

I quietly moved down the hall, easily catching up to his slower pace. "John—"

He jumped, gave a surprised shout, and practically tripped into me as he spun around.

"Easy," I said, putting my hands out to steady him. "I didn't mean to startle you."

"Rory… sorry… I didn't hear you." He cleared his throat and squared his round shoulders.

"You're leaving early," I observed, making it a point

to check my watch.

"Am I?" John started walking again.

I followed him. "Can we talk for a moment?"

"Not really. I've got to see a man about a horse." He turned to the elevator panel on the wall.

I reached over John's shoulder and covered the buttons with the palm of my hand. "I am not the person to do that with."

John huffed. He leaned back to look around me, confirmed the hall was empty, and then said, "I have a standing date every Wednesday."

"With who?"

"Irrelevant. They're not in the industry." John made a shooing motion at my hand.

I didn't budge.

"Mr. Byrne," he said in an authoritative tone oddly reminiscent of the one every high school teacher seemed to possess. "I see a lovely young man Wednesdays at 8:00 p.m. And he charges whether or not I show up on time. Now, do you mind?" John asked with growing frustration.

First Nate. Now John. Am I the only one—

The unbridled and unfinished thought felt as startling as being doused in ice water. Quite suddenly I was— what? Offended? Disappointed? Not exactly. Because I could literally not care any less how John conducted himself in private.

The realization had nothing to do with John.

Nothing to do with Nate, even.

And everything to do with me.

The stark truth was, I was a good—*damn good*—investigator. But I'd never once been able to stop looking for deception, even in my own love life. I sabotaged myself. Went out of my way to isolate myself. To lose myself in the job.

Zero drama. Maximum efficiency.

My life was fulfilled.

But was it… *happy*?

I physically jerked at the notion, as if it were the painful sting of some venomous creature.

John was staring hard, brow furrowed. "Are you okay?"

"Yes," I lied. I moved my hand and pressed the elevator button.

The doors opened, but John was still giving me a doubtful expression.

"I'm fine," I insisted. I reached my arm out over John's head so the doors wouldn't close. "You're going to be late."

"Shit. Right." And just like that, John was done worrying about me. He quickly boarded the elevator.

I stepped in beside him, chose the ground floor, and said as the doors slid shut, "I have some concerns regarding a crew member."

"You found the thief?" John exclaimed.

"No." I looked sideways. "It's about Mr. Lefkowitz."

"Ethan? What about him?"

"What time did he arrive on set Monday morning?"

"Eight o'clock."

"Positive?"

John looked annoyed. "Yes, of course. I met him at the elevator, in fact. We walked onto set together."

So Ethan hadn't arrived before John to grab the script that morning.

"I witnessed some disconcerting behavior today," I said next. "I know this is unrelated to my investigation, but—" I took a moment to collect my thoughts. John already seemed upset. *Tread carefully.* "Ethan appeared to have caused a fair amount of discomfort to your talent while on set today."

"What? No! He's a little intense, I do agree with you there," John babbled, waving a hand. "But he's the real deal. Raw. Powerful. He's got a vision for—"

"I'm only asking that you keep an eye on him."

The doors opened.

John stepped out first, shaking his head and pulling out those silly wraparound earmuffs from his coat pocket. "I will, but believe you me, he's one of the good guys."

"I can't *not* investigate certain people, simply because you insist," I replied, stepping out after him. "The investigation loses integrity that way."

John started for the front doors while saying, "I'll worry about Ethan. You worry about—Marion!"

Said man appeared as we turned the corner. He stood in front of the glass doors, bundled in his winter coat. He raised his mouth from the folds of his scarf, politely greeting John. And unlike earlier, when I might as well have been invisible on set, Marion's gaze zeroed in on me like a gunshot to the chest.

"Get home safe, honey," John told Marion as he brushed past and opened the doors.

"Yes, you too, John," Marion called. He never took his eyes off me.

This man was not making my job easy.

The cold air from outside ruffled Marion's hair before the doors fell shut. He smiled and said, "I washed my hands earlier. Must have missed you."

"Sorry about that. I was bonding with the Key PA."

"Davey. Did you braid his beard?"

I laughed. "Had a smoke."

"Are you two BFFs now?"

"No. He still hates me."

Marion clucked his tongue. His eyes glimmered, and I *knew* I was being laughed at.

"What're you doing?" I asked him.

Marion jutted a thumb over his shoulder at the doors. "Waiting for my ride." He added after a brief pause, "You weren't outside. I didn't think you'd left yet, so I waited here."

Fuck. This wasn't fair. And *that,* in and of itself, was a childish thought, fueled by nothing but primal desire and frustrating, professional limitations. I'd never been so keenly attracted to someone as I was to Marion. Every man I'd been with, from the onset, I knew—hell, *expected*—to be an ex. But I didn't feel that inevitable finale when I stared at Marion's sweet, charming face.

And that I was thinking about a tomorrow with him when there wasn't even a now was absurd.

When had I become this? A man brought to his knees by a bit of harmless flirting from someone a decade younger. It had to be some instinctual, rebellious action because my brain knew I couldn't have Marion. Because there was a case. Boundaries between us. And after I wrapped everything up, the only place I'd see Marion would be on television reruns.

Except… that hurt.

Hurt like hell to think about.

"Don't stop flirting." Marion's voice broke through the cascade of self-deprecating thoughts. "I was having fun."

I could lose my job—my career—by screwing around with him. And yet, the foundation of the wall between us was eroding as if having been battered by relentless tides for a century. Right now, *right here*, I could so easily convince myself to have fun tonight.

John had made it clear he didn't want me treating Marion Roosevelt as a suspect. Did I even believe him to be one?

No.

Not really.

Not at all, actually.

Marion was an actor. He gave no hints that he desired to be anything else. He appeared to love what he did. Marion was a darling to John, to the rest of the cast, to all of the crew. Even some lowly, nobody PA on his first day.

And to top it all off, he clearly had unresolved issues with Ethan, who'd made my lifelong shit list.

He deserved to have his kindness returned.

I stepped closer and carefully leaned into his space.

He didn't move away.

So I kissed his smooth cheek.

Marion studied the linoleum floor. "That was the sweetest letdown I've ever had."

"I'm sorry," I whispered.

He looked up. "I thought for sure I had a chance to figure out who Rory Byrne was."

"It's not you."

"Ah." Marion shrugged a little. Smiled a little. Broke my heart a little. "They always say that."

I touched his chin. Just a fingertip. But he looked at me again. "It's *not* you," I reiterated. I kissed his mouth. Soft full lips worked in contrast to the hard lines of Marion's jawline and cheekbones.

I backed away.

And left.

I recycled empty Altoids tins.

They could be turned into basically anything.

I sat at the table, Optivisor pulled down over my glasses as I stripped the ends of two cables to solder onto a panel small enough to fit into the box. This was the third solar-powered USB charger I'd built since getting home.

The television murmured on the other side of the room. Some show called *New York, New York*. I didn't know anything about it beyond: canned laughter sitcom and Marion Roosevelt's first big break. According to IMDb, anyway. He'd come out in real life after the second season aired, à la Ellen DeGeneres, so said one comment. Marion was several years younger, practically baby-faced. But he still knew how to steal the camera in every scene.

"Jack's gay?" a woman asked, question delivered in over-the-top comedic acting.

I glanced up, raised the visor, and watched Jack—Marion's character—sink into a couch as two friends argued on either side of him.

"Did you not just see the man attached to Jack's face? It was like something out of Alien," the second actor countered.

Insert audience laughter.

She looked down at Jack. *"Is this true?"*

Jack stared up at her. *"You know how you hate my*

dad jokes?"

"Yeah."

"When I have a family, my kids will hate them twice as much."

More laughter.

Marion was a good comedian, even when he had a shitty script to work with.

I heard the *schiiik* of a key being inserted into the front-door lock, and turned in time to see the apartment door open and my most recently acquired ex step inside. I took off the visor as I quickly stood. "Nate?"

"Hi, honey." He shut the door.

I held my hand out. "Key."

Nate ignored the demand, unbuttoned his coat, and walked to the couch while watching the flickering TV screen. "Are you really watching this show?" He picked up the remote from one of the cushions and turned the television off. "It's awful."

"It's not bad," I countered.

Nate turned toward me, rolling his eyes. "And if I'd said it was great, you'd have said it was shit."

"Why are you here?" I asked sternly.

He approached, drew close, and placed his hands low on my hips. "We broke up."

"Right."

"So—"

"I'm not interested."

Nate blindly reached down to grope me through my jeans. "You feel interested."

I grabbed his wrist and pulled his hand away. "Not with you."

He huffed and stepped back. "You have something more pressing to do than getting some no-strings-attached sex?" Nate laughed and held his hands up to interrupt anything I may have tried to say. "*Sorry.* I forgot. You're too busy working. What's the investigation this week? Undercover work as a drummer for some punk band that meets in mom's basement?" He motioned to the worn-out clothes I was still wearing from all day on set. "And what about next week? CPA? Stock trader on Wall Street? Living out of your car while you track—"

"*Nate.*"

"You need to get a fucking life," he shouted.

"Did you come here to fight with me?" I asked calmly.

He might as well have not heard me. "I think it's disconcerting," Nate began, "that in the three months we dated I never knew what in your closet was actually something *Rory Byrne* would wear to the grocery store."

I crossed my arms over my chest, keenly aware of the defensive posture I was taking with him. "I have my groceries delivered."

Nate raised his hands like he wanted to wrap them around my throat. "Your only friend is a cat. Your one hobby is studying wiring diagrams. Every scenario that doesn't play out according to the Dupin Decree, you say fuck it. You only live once and *this is it*?" He looked around the room—a bachelor pad in every sense—and snorted.

I pointed at Nate and said in a collected tone, "I have one rule I live by."

"That's bullshit and you know it. Your life is defined by a rulebook, Rory. You enforce *no lying*, which is pretty fucking ironic considering that's all you do for a living. I mean—who are you? *Really?* So I screwed around. But in our three months, were you ever once *yourself* with me?" Nate reached into his coat pocket and threw the house key at me.

I caught it against my chest and watched him storm to the door. "Hey—"

"Get bent." He slammed the door behind him.

INT. CHAPTER SIX - DAY

I didn't sleep Wednesday night because of Talking Heads.

The band, that is.

"This Must Be the Place" was running on a nonstop loop in my mind, which considering I'd probably last heard that song in 1988… I don't know. I couldn't even remember the lyrics properly.

Something about no money. Always for love.

La, la, la… find me or you?

No.

Did I find you?

Something like that.

But it wasn't a coincidence—being stuck wide-awake in bed, humming the tune to an uncertain and uncomfortable love song while I mentally tended to the wounds Nate burned into my heart. In the solitude and darkness of night, I couldn't dispute his accusations. I used my profession as a yardstick, keeping at bay anything and everything that threatened to make me lose control.

To such an extreme, that I had instead lost my *life*.

Nate was right.

I didn't have friends. I didn't take in the sights of the city. I didn't take a chance on the guy flashing enough signals that he could have landed a jumbo jet, because… why? I'd seen enough shitty human behavior over the last twenty years and wanted to protect myself? At the cost of not experiencing love at all?

I guess, in a sense, I *was* a professional liar. And it was fucking screwed up that I could spin an untrue story to Marion as quickly and easily as breathing, but I couldn't have a drink with the man because my job said no—*he* might be *lying*.

It was barely after seven in the morning, but I was already stalking through staging. Past crafty, I turned down the back corridor and walked along the hall of dressing rooms. I stopped outside the closed door marked with Marion's name and knocked loudly before I could stop myself.

Before I could doubt myself.

"Come in," came a muffled response.

I grabbed the knob and opened the door. Feeble,

wintry sunlight was peeking in through partially closed blinds. An early morning talk show whispered from the television mounted on the wall. Marion stood in front of a full-length mirror, tugging suspenders over his shoulders.

He turned, looked surprised. "Rory—"

I shut the door, walked across the room, took Marion's face into my hands, and leaned down to kiss him. He opened to it without question, without coaxing. He tasted of coffee and something sweet—like pancakes and syrup. Marion drew his hands up my biceps, squeezed, and then settled them around my neck.

He fit against my body as if he were made for no man but me.

I broke the kiss, drew back enough to touch my nose against his, then pressed our foreheads together. "I made mistake."

"Did you?"

"Last night. I shouldn't have…." I leaned back a little, stared at his mismatched eyes. "Think we could do another take?"

Marion's mouth quirked, then broke into a wide smile. "Lights."

"Camera."

"*Action.*"

"Can I take you out for drinks tonight?" I asked.

"I'd love that."

I kissed his mouth again, sealing the deal.

There was a loud knock at the door, followed by Ethan calling Marion's name.

Marion dropped his hands from me and took a quick look around the tiny room. "Shit." He moved to the standing shower, pulled the curtain back, and motioned me inside. "Get in. You're fired if he finds you in here."

I wanted to say, screw Ethan. Wanted to tell Marion then and there I wasn't a PA and not to worry about me. But even if I was going to throw caution to the wind and take him out tonight, I'd still been hired to do a job. It was one thing to blow my cover with Marion, and another entirely with a hothead I couldn't trust like Ethan.

I obediently climbed into the shower and pulled the curtain. I listened to Marion open the door, quickly followed by the scuff of steps and someone backing into a chair, wooden legs dragging across the linoleum.

"I don't have it," Marion said without prompting.

"Then what the fuck are you doing?"

"I'm getting ready for my job, Ethan," Marion said firmly.

The sound of bodily wrestling nearly undid me—the thought of Ethan trying to manhandle Marion against his will making me see red. My heart pounded in my throat as I debated for a split second whether to jump out of the stall and smash his face in with my fist.

"I made you," Ethan hissed. "And I can ruin you. Don't forget that."

Another shove, and this time it sounded as if Marion

hit the floor. Steps drew close to the shower, continued past, and retreated out of the dressing room. The door slammed shut.

I left the stall in a rush to find Marion sitting on the floor. His knees were partially drawn to his chest. "Did he hurt you?" I bent down, took his hands, and pulled Marion to his feet in one quick, fluid motion.

"I'm fine."

I barely heard him over the roar of blood pumping in my ears. I took his face into my hands, inspecting him for any visible damage. "What did he want?" I asked, tone severe and clipped as I struggled with unexpected anger.

"Nothing," Marion insisted. "Please—don't worry about it." He put his hands over mine, pulled them away, and stood on his toes to kiss me. "He's an arrogant asshole. I can handle Ethan."

Marion was lying.

I didn't need deception training to know that.

I'd left Marion alone at his insistence that he was quite fine and needed to get into makeup. But I wasn't happy. At all. Which is why when I came around the corner and saw John at crafty, I made a beeline for him at the expense of the actual task I was being paid to do.

"John. We need to talk," I said when I reached his side.

John looked sideways as he filled a cup with coffee from the airpot. "Oh. You've got an update?"

"No." I shook my head.

"You've got to give me something," he murmured, grabbing a handful of Sweet'N Low packets. "I'm going stir-crazy."

He was not getting any names. Not until I had my Hercule Poirot moment. Because the second John knew about any suspicions I might have, he'd act differently around those individuals. It wouldn't be his fault—human nature and all. But if the thief was smart, the change in John's behavior would be the warning bell to get the hell out of Dodge before I was able to pin them to the wall.

"I'm considering several individuals," I answered. "And that's all I can say at this moment."

"I don't like being told no," John remarked, dumping the artificial sweetener into the black coffee. He stirred the concoction with a plastic spoon before giving me another look.

"You'll like a compromised investigation even less."

"Then what did you want to talk about?" His voice dropped to an almost inaudible whisper when a few crew members entered the staging area from behind us before retreating to the art department's workshop. John took a sip of coffee, made a disgusted face, and started walking away.

I caught up with him in a few easy strides. "Ethan," I said.

"Didn't we discuss him last night?"

"We did," I agreed, following John into the hall and on toward the production office.

"Then why are we revisiting an old conversation?"

"I'm sorry you don't want to hear this, but the reality is, he's a caustic—"

"Randy," Laura exclaimed as we approached her desk. She looked to have just arrived herself, taking off her coat and shoving her purse into a drawer. Her lips were an almost neon pink today.

I paused midstep. "*Rory*," I corrected.

She waved a hand, picked up a sheet of paper with the other, and held it out. "Close enough. I need a hundred copies of tomorrow's sides. Distro when you're done."

"*What?*"

"I've got to make a phone call," John said as a means of excusing himself.

"Hold on—John!" I said after him.

"I need these right away," Laura interrupted.

Fuck.

I took the sheet from her with a snap of my wrist and walked past her desk as John shut his office door. The same young man—the fellow PA who'd been forever relegated to office duties—glanced my way from where he was once again leaning against the top of the copier. He took note of the paperwork I held, then pointed down the long, dim hall.

"The other—"

"Slow as hell, I know," I muttered, marching by.

I passed the closed office doors, the darkened editing suite, and went to the lone photocopier in the unused portion of office space. It was especially eerie in the morning, with hardly a sliver of weak sunlight reaching between the tightly drawn blinds on windows. I opened the top of the machine, put the sheet down on the glass, tapped buttons more forcefully than necessary, and took a step away as the copier coughed to life.

I hadn't even made it to the tenth copy when a prickle of discomfort began to make itself known, tip-tapping along my spine and causing the hair on my neck stand on end. I glanced to the right. Lights and the voices of staffers seemed so far away, encased safely in a bubble I was given no access to. I looked to my left, studying the dark expanse, the nothingness broken only by the shapes of haphazardly placed furniture.

I wasn't alone.

Taking another step back from the copier, I walked farther into the shadows, to the very end of the room, and took a peek around the corner where construction tarps blocked access.

Nothing and no one.

But the distinct edge of uneasiness was still there. Like a dull blade digging between my shoulder blades. I took a few careful steps through the office space before the loud crackle of an open walkie shattered the silence.

"Anyone got eyes on Davey?" the voice of a crew member came through.

I followed the tinny sound into the farthest corner of the room.

Davey was dead on the floor, unwrangled phone cable wrapped around his neck.

INT. CHAPTER SEVEN - DAY

"Rory Byrne," a plainclothes officer said as he was shown into a conference room inside *The Bowery*'s office. He reached a hand out. "It's been a hot minute."

"A few years," I agreed, quickly shaking Detective Harrison Grey's hand.

Grey was about my age. He looked like James Bond—the Craig Someone-Or-Other one—although he was a bit more rumpled around the edges. Then again, anyone would look like they were slumming it when compared to a Hollywood actor wearing custom-tailored Tom Ford suits. A lifetime ago we'd been briefly acquainted, but like all my relationships, it'd gone the way of the dodo. *Unlike* the rest of my exes though, we'd severed ties amicably and kept in touch professionally.

"What the hell mess you get involved with now?" Grey asked. He turned and watched through the glass wall as a medical examiner, flanked by uniformed cops, wheeled a gurney down the hall.

John and Laura were hot on their heels before the producer gave an instruction that sent Laura to make phone calls at her desk, directly across from us. Damage control for the production, no doubt. John disappeared out of view as he rushed after the ME.

Grey looked at me again.

"Theft," I stated. "John Anderson is my client."

Grey put a hand on the back of a chair and inclined his head in the direction of the ME's plus one. "So was *that* an unfortunate coincidence or relevant to your case?"

"The victim was actually my number-one person of interest," I answered, keeping one eye on Laura over Grey's shoulder. "So I'd say it's pretty relevant."

"Sorry."

I crossed my arms and leaned back against the far wall. "It obviously wasn't him."

"Hmm. What's this do for your pool of suspects?"

"I've still got a few."

Two, really. Ethan Lefkowitz was going to remain a suspect until I could piece together his hostility toward talent—Marion especially. And Laura Turner, based on the fact that she flanked John's office, that I'd not been able to prove her innocence via the current timetables, and that she harbored an intense dislike for set crew in particular, which was decidedly strange.

Grey took out a notepad from his coat. "Mind if we play Twenty Questions?"

"Please do. I'm still undercover and may be able to salvage this case."

He shot me an amused smile. "You'd have made a better cop, you know."

I shrugged and adjusted my glasses. "I don't like guns."

Grey set his pen to paper. "What time did you get in?"

"Around 7:15 a.m."

"And you found the victim when?"

I pulled back the sleeve of my shirt and checked the time. "Around 7:30 a.m.; Davey—the deceased—has a 7:00 a.m. call-time. I didn't check in with him when I arrived, so I'm not sure what his movements were prior to death."

Grey took a folded sheet out of his pocket and waved it idly. "Mr. Anderson has already provided me with this."

I pushed off the wall and snatched the paper. It was cast and crew call-times for that Thursday. "Can I borrow your pen?" I took the offering, leaned over the table, and began to cross off names. "John is not a suspect. Mr. Roosevelt was in his dressing room—"

"Marion Roosevelt," Grey agreed, watching me

mark up the list. "He looks hot as hell in the promos for this show. Is he really as short as they say he is?"

I glanced at Grey over the rim of my glasses. "Yes," I answered brusquely, returning to the call-times. "Mr. Lefkowitz… I had, well, ears on him." *Unfortunately.* I circled a few more names and handed back the paper. "These ones with circles—you've got a few PAs who may have seen Davey come through the office. And he was certainly with someone, unless he strangled himself." I said that last part dryly.

"He might have," Grey stated.

I shook my head. "No. This was a murder."

"When folks have a mind to end it, they find a way."

"This isn't a suicide," I insisted.

Grey stared at me for a beat, offered a sympathetic expression, then said, "The ME will decide that. In the meantime, I'm going to have to shut down production, at least for today. I've got to get CSU down here to comb over the scene."

"That's highly problematic for me."

"A death trumps robbery, Byrne."

I could hear John speaking, his voice bouncing off the walls of staging as the remaining office staff and I were escorted from the area by the police. I poked my head into the doorway to see him addressing the entire cast and crew from set. Every single person listened in utter silence. I stepped quietly into the massive room, moved closer, and identified a few fellow PAs among the crowd. Grief-stricken, confused, one was even crying.

The reactions of those immediately under Davey's power-tripping little fingers all appeared sincere in their upset. Good for them—they weren't suspects in the murder as far as I was concerned. Bad for me—because they weren't suspects in the murder.

"Rory," someone whispered.

I quickly turned to my left and looked down at Marion. His expression was disorganized heartache and a failing attempt at remaining stoic. "You okay?" I murmured.

He nodded, indicated toward John, and stepped closer to me.

John was saying, "The police have informed me that we will be closed down for the day." The crew finally began to mutter among one another. "People—*people*! Please. I know this is unprecedented. There's a deadline for the show, folks are working under contracts, and we all need our paychecks. But we are obligated to accommodate the needs of New York's finest as they investigate what happened to one of our own."

"How'd he die?" someone asked.

"I heard he hanged himself," another called.

John put both hands up. Even from the back of the throng, I could see his round face breaking out in a sweat. "We all want answers," he insisted loudly over the raised voices. "But it can't come from us. We must let the police do their job so we can come back and do ours and make Davey proud with a complete season of *The Bowery*."

"This is like that *Supernatural* episode," someone in front of me muttered.

"The what?" a coworker whispered back.

"Where on-set deaths finally shut down production, but really no one cares, they just want to do their job. It was a funny one."

"Dude. Davey is dead."

"*I know.*"

I felt Marion take my hand into his own, squeezing tightly.

John continued, "Don't call us, we'll call you." He reached into a pocket for his handkerchief. "And we will all get back to work as soon as humanly possible."

Marion let go of my hand as cast and crew began to turn around and head toward the door immediately behind us. He took a deep breath and ran his fingers through his hair. "A hell of a day, and it's hardly ten," he said, eyes cast down. His face had a decidedly gray shade to it. "I guess this puts a damper on our drinks."

I started to agree. Because that would have been following the rules. "*No,*" I abruptly answered.

Marion looked up. "No?" he repeated, confused.

"No," I said again. "We—we should still go out."

He raised one finely shaped eyebrow.

"You only live once."

Marion cracked a smile. "That's true, I suppose." He looked at the folks shuffling around us to the doorway to go home, then nodded. "All right. Let me change out of costume."

"Sure. I'll be here." I watched Marion head in the opposite direction of the crowd, pass crafty, and disappear down the side hall. I retrieved my phone from my pocket, walked to the far corner for a bit of privacy, and dialed Violet Shelby.

"Morning, Rory," she answered. Never *good morning*. Shelby was a realist.

"Ma'am, there's been a situation."

"Report."

"Murder. Well, I'm certain it will be a murder once the ME files the paperwork." I glanced over my shoulder at the handful of folks left standing around John. "Davey—Key PA. He was my first boss in the film hierarchy."

"Was he a suspect?"

"My most likely candidate."

Shelby muffled a curse. "What happened?"

"It's unclear. There's a branch off the production office that's unused due to partial renovation. I found him in the corner on the floor, a bunch of phone cords wrapped around his neck."

"Jesus. How're *you*?"

"Fine, ma'am."

"Yeah?"

"It's not my first dead body. I'm okay, really. But it throws a hell of a wrench into the works. Davey had motive, means, and he even talked about a recently acquired project that was going to get him into the big leagues."

"Guilty innocence," Shelby said thoughtfully, almost to herself.

"The police are shutting down production for the day," I continued. "Someone killed him. I know it. And that person works for the show. There's a chance it's unrelated to the theft, but given my own belief that Davey possessed the missing script, I don't put much stock into these being two distinct events."

"I'm inclined to agree. Listen, Rory… you be careful. Someone at Kaufman is so desperate for their fifteen minutes, they're willing to lie, steal, and kill. If your cover is blown—"

"It won't be," I said with absolute certainty. "Twenty years, ma'am. Have some faith in me."

"I've never doubted you."

I looked toward John again. He was mopping his face with the handkerchief while talking with Ethan and two other department heads. The director's body language was interesting. He was rigid. Taut, like a rubber band about to snap. Ethan spoke with his hands, gesturing with concentrated intensity. I took a few steps to the side to change my angle. Ethan's pant leg was discolored over his right knee, and a dusty white clung to the material.

"Rory?" Shelby's voice in my ear jerked me back to the conversation.

"Sorry. What was that?" I turned away, saw Marion returning in street clothes.

"I want you to keep me updated. I'll phone Anderson, but let me—"

"I will," I said hastily. "I need to go, ma'am."

"Good luck," she said and ended the call without another word.

I put my phone in my pocket, fetched my coat from the crew lockers nearby, and pulled my arms through as Marion shot me a smile while walking past me. I discreetly followed him out of staging, down the hall, and to the elevator. We rode to the first floor in silence, stepped out the front doors and into the now-bright, crisp-cold morning.

"Do you like beer?" Marion asked.

"For breakfast?"

He laughed a little, looked up at me, and squinted one eye as the sun hit him just right. "Steinway Bierhaus is only two blocks from here. They serve a mean pint-and-pretzel combo."

"This is a film neighborhood," I started. "You don't mind being seen out with a guy?"

"I think the industry as a whole would be more shocked if I was out with a woman."

I stopped at the end of the block. "You know what

I mean."

"Not if you don't care."

It felt liberating to say, "I don't."

We walked the rest of the way in a comfortable, companionable silence. Marion kept his hands tucked into his pockets, shoulder bumping into me now and again. I took a deep breath of cold air scented with exhaust, garbage, and road salt, then draped my arm across his shoulders. Marion tucked into my side. Warm and perfect.

A feeling of respite came over me. A calmness and gentleness that in all my forty-plus years I couldn't ever recall experiencing quite like this moment. That it was okay to need this—human touch and tenderness—even in the midst of a job. *Despite* the job. I could uncover a thief, stop a killer, and still take a moment to love a man.

I could take a moment to live.

We entered Steinway Bierhaus, and a *whoosh* of warm air hit my face. I followed Marion up the steps from the front door. He gave a friendly hello to a man putting away glasses at a bar well stocked with high-end spirits, then led the way into a large communal drinking hall. Multiple big-screen televisions were turned on, each playing a different sports channel. A scattering of customers sat on benches at the long tables, mostly eating, but a few shared pitchers of beer while glued to a hockey game.

Marion stopped at a counter on one end of the room, ordered for us both, and insisted on paying. I took the glasses of beer and followed him to a table near the back windows that was completely empty. He set the basket of hot pretzels and mustard down, unbuttoned his coat, and piled the winter garments beside him on the seat. I sat next to him and slid a beer over.

Marion accepted the drink, considered for a moment, then raised it. "To Davey."

I nodded and tapped my glass against his.

Marion took a sip and said, "It isn't selfish to not want to think about it, is it?"

"No," I quickly answered. "Dwelling on death never helped anyone."

He reached for a pretzel. "I never would have guessed you were a PA when I first saw you." Marion dunked one end into the container of mustard and took a bite. "I noticed you on set, when you first arrived."

"Did you?"

"You carry a lot of confidence." He sucked the salt off his thumb and then motioned to his shoulders. "Here. But you weren't dressed like a producer. I thought, perhaps a stand-in gaffer for an episode."

"Why's that?"

"They're usually big guys like you." Marion reached for my hand, turned it palm up, and stroked my fingers. "But when I shook your hand—too soft."

"You *are* observant," I answered, my heart thudding hard.

"I told you," Marion said with that cute grin. "I've

been racking my brain, trying to figure out what you did before deciding to toss your hat into the film industry." He tore off another bite-size piece of pretzel, coated it liberally in mustard, and ate it. "It wasn't a physical-labor job."

I shook my head. "No."

"But not paper-pushing like an accountant either."

"No."

"So what?"

I turned my hand over to cover his. "Promise me it remains between us?"

The delight in Marion's face waned a little, but he tried for a casual tone. "Was it porn?"

I laughed. "Definitely not."

"All right. I'm officially stumped."

"I don't work in the film industry. I'm not really a PA."

Marion cocked his head. "I'm confused."

"I'm a private investigator. I'm working undercover on set." I removed my wallet before Marion could ask another question, and showed him my PI license. "I work for Dupin Private Investigations."

The blood had all but drained from Marion's face. "Why—I mean—what are you investigating?"

I snapped my wallet shut. "A theft."

"Theft?" he echoed in a whisper.

"Of a script."

"The—*John's* script?"

My heart missed a beat. "You know about that?"

Marion stared at his beer. He rubbed his hands up and down his thighs. "He's talked about it."

"To who?"

But Marion shook his head. "It was at our Christmas party. John was drunk—first time I'd ever seen him have more than one glass. He doesn't hold his drink very well." Marion glanced at me. "John told me about it. He might have said something to James, my costar. I… I mentioned it in passing to Ethan. I don't know if John told anyone else at the party."

I shifted on the bench, put a leg on either side, and took Marion's hand in mine. I gave it a firm squeeze. "I need to know who'd steal that script."

"I don't know."

"Marion—"

"I don't," he insisted. His hand was clammy. "Why would I?"

"Because you're perceptive."

"It wasn't me," he said hastily. "I would never."

"I know it wasn't you." After a pause, I asked, "But did Ethan?"

Marion's head jerked, and he looked at me. "No."

"Why are you lying about Ethan? You've been covering his behavior and protecting others since I met you."

"Don't worry about—"

"I have to," I replied. "He's a suspect."

Marion pulled his hand free, shifted to mimic my sitting position so that our knees bumped together, and said, "Ethan is an asshole. But I'm telling you, if that script is already missing, it's not because of him."

That was the truth.

A truth stuck in the middle of lies, but a truth nonetheless.

Marion reached up, scrubbed his face with both hands, and blinked his pretty eyes a few times. "I need this show," he said, voice low. "I can't give up Tommy's character. Being able to lose myself in him. He—he loves with a love that is more than love."

"Poe."

Marion flashed a weak smile. "There's a dichotomy to Tommy's character. He can be violent. Cruel, even. It's a cathartic experience I need."

"Why?" I dared to question.

"Because I'm angry," Marion said, as if it were an admission of guilt. "And Tommy O'Sullivan gives me a constructive outlet to work through some shit."

"We all get angry."

Marion snorted. "We didn't all date Ethan Lefkowitz." He stared at me, and the grim line of his kissable mouth said a lot about what my facial reaction must have been. "So even if it means running interference and taking the brunt of his anger, fine. But I won't have this show taken away from me. I'm doing my best to keep James on for another season as it is. He's been thinking of quitting the industry altogether. It's important, you know?"

"What is?"

"That viewers see Tommy and Hugh together forever. It matters. To people like us. Doesn't it?"

My shoulders dropped a bit. I slipped my hands around Marion's wrists, petting his forearms. "It matters," I agreed.

"I understand you've been hired to do a job," he continued. "But please—don't do anything that would jeopardize this show."

"My ex," I murmured.

Marion glanced up. "What about him?"

"He made me angry too."

"Why? I mean, besides being an ex."

I slid my hands free, reached behind me for my peacoat, and removed the folded grocery list I'd been carrying for three days. I offered it to Marion.

He unfolded the note and laughed a little. "Oh… *Rory*."

"I broke up with him in a text."

"Did he run over your mother?" Marion asked, his chuckle growing a bit stronger, more authentic.

"He broke my one rule."

"Which is?"

"Don't lie."

Marion sobered again. "Even a white lie?"

"If I fuck up the pancakes but you don't want to discourage my culinary interests, that's one thing. But if you lie and I catch you, I can't forgive that."

"I'd never deter a man from pursuing the perfect pancake." He folded the note, still staring at me. "Are you over your ex?"

"Oh yeah." I reached out, touched Marion's smooth cheek, traced an eyebrow. "Are you over yours?"

He tore the dipshit note into several pieces and tossed the confetti onto the tabletop. "I'm onto bigger and blonder things."

"Have you ever been to the Observation Deck of the Empire State Building?"

Marion looked particularly confused at the sudden subject shift. "*No*...." he drew out, almost as if it were a question.

"Me neither," I said. "I've lived here my entire life, and I've never gone to the top."

"So?"

I looked at the table, picked up my beer, and took a sip. "So let's do it."

INT. CHAPTER EIGHT - NIGHT

Wind in our hair on the eighty-sixth floor.

Bags of honey-roasted Nuts 4 Nuts.

Shopping at Macy's.

Too many Manhattans at dinner.

Caresses and kisses in the taxi to my apartment.

By nightfall, I was at the mercy of my own uninhibited desire. An animalistic lust so visceral, so *ancient*, it seemed to vibrate outward from the marrow of my bones. My entire body thrummed like a musical instrument. And every chord, every note, played only for Marion.

Coats lay scattered down the hallway in our wake. Marion bumped into the bedroom doorframe, then the door. His arms were wrapped around my neck, mouth hard and insistent on my own. I shoved the door open with one hand and used my body to push Marion into the room. He hit the foot of the bed with the back of his legs and went down with a drunken laugh, taking me with him. I pressed my thigh against his crotch, threaded our fingers together to hold his hands above his head, and sucked hard on Marion's neck.

He gasped, writhed, thrust up against my thigh. "*Rory.*"

I let up on his neck, moved my hands to the hem of his long-sleeve shirt, and yanked it to his chest. Marion sat up so I could finish pulling it over his head. I wrenched myself free from my own shirt, and then pulled Marion up and against my chest.

Flesh-to-flesh.

Soft skin, flexing muscles, and the unmistakable hardness of a man's body pressed so intimately against my own turned the flame inside me into a wildfire.

There was no stopping this.

Not until it burned me whole.

Marion shoved his hand between us, fondled me through my worn jeans, and whispered against my lips, "I want you to take me."

I moved my hands under Marion's ass and flipped him onto his back again. He let out another boyish laugh, and then it was a race to see who could unbutton their jeans the quickest. I leaned over to the nightstand, knocked off my alarm clock, hit the switch to the custom LED installation I'd built, and accidently set the room alight in muted, shifting-color palettes.

"Shit." I finally grabbed the handle on the drawer, opened it, and took out a box of condoms.

"Are we fucking inside a rainbow?" Marion laughed.

"Sorry, I—"

"Keep it on."

I found the lube and turned to look at him. The room was still dark, but the colored lights mounted to the corners of the walls and along the ceiling bathed Marion's naked body in soft, glowing hues of alternating reds, blues, purples, and greens. He met my look, grinned, and rolled onto his stomach in blatant invitation.

I got behind Marion, leaned over him, and we passed several drunken moments probing and stretching and caressing until he was a supple, quivering mess underneath me.

"R-Rory," he pleaded, sounding next to tears. "Not yet. Not like this."

I removed my fingers and smoothed his asscheek with one hand. I shushed him, murmured sweet words against his neck as I kissed and sucked his skin. Marion's voice cracked and hitched. He arched his back and rubbed his ass against my pelvis.

I pushed back to meet him. "Think you're ready?"

"Please," he begged. "Be rough. I like it."

I could do that.

Sitting up, I opened a condom and rolled it over

myself. With one hand holding the base of my cock and the other firmly planted between Marion's shoulder blades, I rocked my hips back and forth until I breached muscles and sank into his gorgeous ass.

"*Jesus.*" I leaned over Marion, got an arm under his chest to hold him flush against me, then shoved hard into the tight heat.

Marion cried loudly. He scrambled for purchase, grabbing at a pillow with one hand and the other reaching back, fingers digging into my hip hard enough to leave marks. "Oh God! Like that!"

I bit Marion's earlobe and murmured, "This what you wanted?"

It's what I've wanted.

"You're so big—don't—don't stop."

I grunted. "You gonna think about my cock tomorrow?"

I'll be thinking of you.

"Yes. Holy shit. Make me feel it." He turned his head, arched his neck, and awkwardly kissed my mouth.

I sped up. The bed squeaked, and Marion's voice was hoarse with screams. "Don't forget who gave you this ride."

I can't not see you again. Please let there be a tomorrow for us.

My muscles burned. My breathing came out in harsh pants. I paused for a brief moment to collect myself.

"Wh-what're you doing?" Marion protested. He

ground his hips roughly against the mattress. "I'm almost there!"

I tilted my head close and kissed him again. "Say my name," I demanded.

Marion looked utterly wild in the psychedelic lighting. His hair was in complete disarray, and his two-toned eyes black, pupils blown wide with hunger and want. "Rory," he said obediently. "*Rory*, please. Let me be the best you've had."

Then he flexed his muscles around my dick, and I groaned. I let go of him, pushed up onto my fists, and used the bed as leverage to screw Marion into next week. Orgasm hit me like a horse kick to the chest.

Powerfully.

Violently.

A release so good, so euphoric, it fucking hurt. An experience like nothing I'd ever had with a partner in all my life. I slid out, lifted Marion's hips, and reached under to help him finish.

But the bed was already wet with his cum.

Beep. Beep. Beep.

I opened my eyes and regretted the decision nearly immediately.

The room was still awash in neon colors.

My mouth tasted like I'd been licking a wet dog. And my head was thudding, each pound a reminder that I was too old to abuse whiskey the way we had last night.

Beep. Beep. Beep.

I rolled over to smack the clock, then remembered it was on the floor. I leaned down, blindly hit a few buttons—which, after I turned the radio on and adjusted the volume to a morning talk show, managed to turn the alarm off.

"Marilyn Monroes are delicious," Marion murmured, his voice slurred as he spoke into a pillow.

"How many did you have?" I asked, gingerly putting a hand to my forehead.

"One bottle of champagne's worth," he answered, still unmoving. "Four ounces per cocktail... so six Monroes. And a dozen maraschino cherries."

"Hedonist."

Marion laughed a little. He rolled onto his back and looked at me. "You look like you got rode hard and put away wet."

"I had several Manhattans."

"I drank more than you."

"I'm a dozen maraschino cherries older too." I slowly sat up, swung my legs over the edge of the bed, and took a moment to gather my balance before I fell off the side of the world. "I can't believe I remembered what apartment I lived in."

"I'm glad this one is yours. Otherwise, whoever owns this bed would be pissed."

I grunted and got to my feet. I felt around the floor a moment, tugged on my jeans from last night, found my glasses, and stumbled out of the room. I made a quick stop in the bathroom, relieved myself, brushed my teeth, and splashed several handfuls of cold water on my face before continuing to the kitchen. My bare chest pimpled from the coolness in the air, and I stopped long enough to adjust the thermostat on the wall.

Gary stood on the kitchen counter, looking harassed, despite the crossed eyes. He meowed loudly and paced back and forth.

"Morning, baby," I kissed his head. "I'm sorry. Daddy had—a night out." I fetched Gary's food, refilled his bowl, and set it beside the water dish.

While the cat ate, coffee brewed and I blundered my way through cooking an entire frying pan full of bacon and eggs. Anything to sop up the last of the alcohol in my system, especially if John ended up calling the crew back to Kaufman today. As the food popped and sizzled, I finally heard Marion leave the bedroom, pad down the hall, and come to a stop at the kitchen doorway in nothing but boxer briefs and my T-shirt from last night, a few sizes too large for him.

"I can't find my shirt," he stated, running his hand through his dated and currently disheveled haircut.

It wasn't until that moment that I understood the whole straight-guy thing—why they loved their girlfriends wearing their too-big-for-them shirts and how their ladies straddled the adorable yet positively fuckable line. Because Marion might have looked as if he was wearing a bag, but it was definitely waking certain bodily responses in me.

"You look better in that."

He gave me a lopsided smile before glancing at the coffee pot. "Mugs?" He pointed to the cupboard above, and I nodded. Marion retrieved two, set them on the counter, then helped himself to the fridge for cream. "John hasn't called, has he?"

I took one of the cups he offered and had a sip before saying, "I don't think so. But if you couldn't find your shirt, I don't have high hopes for my phone."

Marion chuckled. He studied the decal on his coffee mug for a beat, looked back at the magnets covering the stainless-steel fridge, then said, "You really like cats."

"I really like cats," I agreed. "Gary's around here somewhere. He doesn't like new people."

Marion poked his head out of the kitchen doorway. "Oh. That would be the sweet, blue-eyed baby giving me stink-eye."

"That's him." I grabbed two plates from the nearby cupboard and started shoveling fried food onto them. I gave Marion one, looked over his shoulder at the table covered in my techy supplies, and cursed.

Marion set the plate on the counter. "Don't worry about it." He hoisted himself up, put his plate in his lap, and took a bite of crispy bacon.

"Sorry," I said. "I'm not used to guys spending the night and staying for a breakfast that should be eaten at a table the next morning."

"Should I have left already?"

I shook my head and put a hand on his bare thigh. "No." I kissed his lips and licked off a flake of bacon.

Marion was staring intensely as I pulled back. "Can I ask you something? Get the serious shit out of the way before it gives me anxiety?"

"All right…."

"Do you regret last night?"

"No," I said again. "Do you?"

Marion quickly shook his head. "But I… like you. I think a lot more than I've let on." He set the plate aside, licked his lips nervously, and put his hands on my chest.

I stared at Marion's bright mismatched eyes. His expression was so human. Not acting human. It wasn't that perfect. It wasn't choreographed or *in the moment*. He didn't know the lines of this scene unfolding before us. His expression faltered, hesitated, but more than anything, there was a vulnerable hopefulness twinkling in those green and brown eyes.

"Go ahead," I prodded.

Marion's fingers tensed a little against my muscles. "Could we do it again? I don't only mean the sex, but yeah, that was good. I mean—all of it. I think yesterday was the best date I've ever had."

I put my hands over Marion's and realized he could feel my heart pounding against my rib cage. I released a breath, and simultaneously, his fingers relaxed. He petted instead of digging his fingers into my flesh.

"It was the best I've had too," I whispered.

INT. CHAPTER NINE - DAY

"Don't you speak that way to me, Tommy O'Sullivan. You might blaspheme in front of the lads, but I ain't one of them," Marion's costar ordered, in character as Hugh.

The entire set was silent. Engrossed. Mesmerized by Marion and James lost in a moment of intensity as longtime lovers. I stood near the back, behind the sound cart with Paul, holding my breath as I watched *Tommy* pace like a caged animal. His agitation and anger were palpable, and the focused conflict between the two men spread outward until every crew member on set seemed to be scratching at some unpleasant itch on their bodies.

As expected, John had been given a conditional all-clear by the NYPD that morning. Department heads phoned crew and cast in for a ten o'clock call-time, which set the production behind schedule about thirteen hours since the day before, but it was better than nothing, I figured. Marion took a taxi from my place to his for a shower and change of clothes, and I, having left my car at the garage in Queens the day before, took the subway into Astoria. The next time I saw Marion since closing the apartment door behind him was in this scene, literally vibrating with negative energy he released through Tommy.

It was one thing to watch such masterful acting on a screen, removed from the moment. But experienced firsthand… frankly, it was overwhelming.

Tommy pushed his suit coat back and settled his hands on his hips as he came to an abrupt stop. He stared at the floor.

Hugh stepped forward, took Tommy by the chin, and had to grab his shoulder when the gang leader physically recoiled. "Stop fightin' me," he whispered.

Tommy's Adam's apple bobbed painfully. He looked up, eyes glossy with unfallen tears of rage. "Some days I hate you," he said in an Irish accent intentionally bastardized to convey years of living in America.

"Aye," Hugh answered with a small nod. "But you love me in the night." He kissed Tommy, hard and aggressive.

"Cut!" Ethan shouted. "Print that!" He stood from his chair.

Paul whistled to himself while removing his headphones. "*Jesus Christ*, can Marion act."

The entire crew seemed to let out a collective breath when the two actors stepped away from one another. The assistant director announced twenty minutes for lights and camera to prep for the next angle. The technicians had a job to do, so no one questioned the directions as they descended onto the scenery. But there was most assuredly a somberness to their moods, and the complexity and seriousness of this scene weren't helping to lighten hearts any. Orders being barked in film-set lingo had a heaviness to them. I hadn't seen many, if any, people smiling or joking so far that day.

"The crew is taking Davey's passing pretty hard," I said, glancing down at Paul.

He leaned back in his chair to stare up at me. "Ah, well, a crew is like a family. Sort of like Thanksgiving. You've got all these competing personalities forced together, and everyone needs to get along and not upset Grandma. You've got that one uncle who has been drinking since noon, and there's also the cousin who brags about everything, and sooner or later you're going to reach over the table and sucker-punch them. But you're still a family. Everyone's saying Davey hanged himself in that back office."

Not true.

But Paul thought it was gospel.

Detective Grey had felt it was a likely scenario too. It wasn't. I was *certain*. But for now, having near a hundred folks think it was self-inflicted was better than them realizing a murderer worked alongside them.

"Who's saying that?" I asked.

Paul shrugged. "I dunno. Everyone."

"I see."

"It's a hell of a way to call it quits," Paul said sadly.

"Rory!"

I looked ahead and toward the left. John was sitting in his chair, phone to one ear, waving for me to come hither.

"I'll be right back," I said, patting Paul's shoulder. I sidestepped a few crew members and frowned as I approached John. "What's wrong?"

He put a hand over the phone's mouthpiece and whisper-spoke, "I need you to do me a quick favor."

"John."

"I know, I know. You're an *I* not an *A*," he said. "But we're really scrambling today."

I crossed my arms and begrudgingly asked, "What do you need?"

"*What?*" John returned his focus to his phone call, leaving me hanging. "No, no. Meredith. … When the NYPD storms the house and shuts production down. … Hopes and dreams aren't a practical insurance."

While waiting for John to tear himself away from the argument he was getting into over money, time, contracts, and whatever other problems producers got paid big bucks to untangle, I shot the actors a quick look. Costar James had taken a seat and accepted a water bottle from someone nearby. A makeup artist joined him to do light touch-ups after the hot and heavy kissing between him and—

I spun around where I stood, looking for Marion. He wasn't standing in Tommy O'Sullivan's parlor, and he wasn't seated with James, who was clearly waiting on the technical setup. I uncrossed my arms, took a few steps backward, and caught Marion speaking with Ethan farther away on the stage. He looked upset—pleading, even. Ethan dug his phone out of a pocket, turned the screen toward Marion, and the younger man sobered considerably at whatever he was staring at. He straightened his shoulders, nodded minutely, and started walking toward the side door.

"Striking!" a big guy's voice bellowed from nearby, and then a massive light turned on and completely blinded me. "PA! Don't look at the light when we call that."

"Yeah," I answered gruffly, blinking away the spots.

John grabbed my arm, another one of those not so subtle bicep appreciation squeezes. "My planner," he murmured, pulling the phone away from his ear very briefly. "On my desk."

With that dismissal from John, I picked my way around people and equipment and left the set. I made a quick detour, turned right, and slipped down the dressing-rooms hallway. I stopped outside Marion's door and knocked gently.

No response.

"Marion?" I called.

Nothing.

I tried the knob, found it unlocked, and the door swung open.

Empty.

Strange. I couldn't imagine he'd go anywhere else when taking the side exit, but maybe he was in the bathroom down the main corridor. Or even sneaked down to the loading dock for a smoke. Either seemed likely, considering the emotional high he'd been on, followed by yet another spat with Herr Director, so I shut the door and continued toward the production office.

"Randy," Laura stated as I entered.

"Rory," I corrected again, not stopping for any handout this time.

"Can I send you on a run?"

"I'm actually doing one for John at the moment, but I'll swing back in a bit," I replied.

Davey's death had really gotten me thinking. The lack of any real crossover between set and office—and what did exist with PAs, Davey and Laura had dissolved by relegating them to one location or the other—suggested to me that his killer worked with him.

That it'd be someone from set.

And that if his death and the missing script were indeed related, the killer could very likely *be* the thief.

Laura was one of my first suspects. She was higher up than Davey. She hadn't liked him. And her petty jealousy of even his lowly set position had been brought to my attention. But she wasn't a cold-blooded killer. That was simply not in her makeup as a human being. And yesterday morning she had only just arrived for the workday when we crossed paths. Her cheeks had still been flushed from the cold, for God's sake. There hadn't been time to overpower a bigger man and strangle him to death.

No. It wasn't her.

Both events originated with someone on set.

I'd stake my reputation on it.

"How many people does John need doing errands for him?" she asked with a shake of her head.

I started to consider that muttered question, but as I stopped outside of John's office and opened the door, the words crumbled like ash from the tip of a cigarette.

Marion jerked his head up. He shut the bottom drawer of John's desk and quickly stood. "R-Rory."

Had he—?

Was he—?

"Wh-what are you doing here?" he stuttered.

I let go of the doorknob.

"*Wait.* It's not what you think." Marion moved around the desk to stop me from leaving.

I took a step back.

"Rory, please." Marion was following me out of the office.

I glanced over my shoulder, and a few of the staffers

were looking up from their desks at us. Taking Marion by the arm, I quickly led him away from the open area, past Laura and the conference room, down the hall, and back to staging.

"Would you let go of me?" Marion protested.

"*No.*" My voice shook with even that one word as I tried to tamp down the rage boiling inside me. I could barely breathe the rest of the walk to his dressing room, which upon reaching, I shoved Marion inside and slammed the door shut behind us. "It was you this entire time?"

Marion swallowed hard and vehemently shook his head. "It wasn't. I swear to God."

"Where's the script, Marion?"

"I don't know!" he cried.

"Then why the hell were you in John's office?" I retorted. I'd been hurt in the past, but this betrayal was akin to my heart being torn from my chest. I was shaking with a mixture of fury and anguish and adrenaline. How could I be so *stupid*.

"It—I was—because of Ethan," he said, voice trembling and lip quivering. Marion looked as if he were about to pass out. "I let him take… pictures. When we were dating."

"What kind of pictures?" I demanded.

Marion looked up. "The kind you blackmail someone over." He wiped angrily at his eyes. "He's refused to delete them, and now he's threatening to give them to tabloids if I don't steal John's script for him."

"You're lying."

"No!"

"I have one rule," I started, and my voice caught again. "I *told* you that."

"I never lied. I didn't tell you about…. Those pictures are humiliating and embarrassing, and I'm trying to deal with the fallout of a bad breakup while working with my ex on a project that means more to me than the air in my lungs. I can't be faulted for that."

"If Ethan has the script—"

"He *doesn't*, Rory," Marion shouted. "You said the script was already stolen. And I told you last night, if it's gone, Ethan doesn't have it. And I know that because he's forcing *me* to do his bidding. He doesn't know it's already gone."

I stared at Marion for an intensely long, unnerving moment. "But you know it's gone."

He nodded weakly.

"Why are you bothering to raid John's private office?"

"For a copy," he admitted. "Or—or anything I could give Ethan to get him to *back off*. I'm desperate to save my career." Tears slipped down his face. "I want to be a man that younger people can look up to. And I can't do that while being plastered on grocery-store tabloids. I can't bear being the face of homophobic jokes and stereotypes." He wiped at his face again with the sleeve of his suit coat. "I'm worth a lot in the industry right now. Ethan wants to be attached to whatever project I take next. I kept telling him no. I wasn't going to abuse John's trust. I wasn't going to be Ethan's ticket to the top. But…."

I took a deep breath, distancing myself from Marion's grief. "Who has the script?"

"*I don't know,*" he said again. "I'm telling you the truth. Until you told me yesterday, I assumed John was still fiddling away at it." Marion reached out, but I stepped back. "Rory—*please.*"

"You've got to do better than that," I answered. "What about Davey?"

Marion's brows knitted together. "What about him?"

"Who killed him?"

"*Killed?* But I heard… people… they're saying he hanged—"

I shook my head.

Marion put a hand over his mouth. He turned quickly, knelt in front of a small desk overlooking the window, and was sick into the trash bin. Instinct took over hurt, and my need to ease Marion's discomfort forced my deadened feet to step forward. I crouched and put a hand on his back, soothing up and down. He wiped his mouth with a shaking hand before gripping the bin again like he feared there'd be a round two.

You couldn't fake this sort of response.

"Would Ethan kill someone?" I asked in a quiet tone. "Even if by accident?"

Not that Davey's death was anything but intentional.

Marion didn't immediately respond, his silence speaking volumes more than his eventual words. "I don't…." He spit into the trash. "I'm not sure."

"Babe."

Marion looked at me again.

"What about James?"

"He'd be the last to steal a script. I'm serious. He's done with the industry. He wants to go into *construction*. Work for his brother's company."

"Then could someone else have overheard your conversations with Ethan? When he's been pressuring you to take the script?"

"No. We spoke in private."

"On set?" I clarified.

"Well, yes, I don't see him anywhere else. But no one would have heard—"

And it was like both of us came to the same startling conclusion at once.

I held my breath.

Marion snapped his mouth shut. He reached to his chest and very delicately touched his tie.

The microphone.

He reached around his back to unclasp the transmitter worn under his coat, which sent the audio wirelessly to Paul's receivers on the sound cart. Marion stared at the buttons for a moment, but I guess after having been wearing the gear for so many years, he knew how to turn them on and off.

"Could Paul have picked up our conversation this far from set?" I asked.

"Yeah, maybe," Marion said with a grimace. He glanced up from the device. "Sound recordists are supposed to turn our mics down between takes—no eavesdropping."

"But?"

"Paul's forgotten in the past. People make mistakes. I thought nothing of it," Marion explained.

I recalled the intense disagreement between Marion and Ethan I'd overheard through headphones the other day, regarding his costar's performance. If what Marion said was true, Paul should have known better then. He should have turned the mics off, especially if Marion had caught him previously doing no such thing. So how often did he listen in on conversations he shouldn't have been privy to?

Had he overheard Ethan's demands for the script? And while Marion was dragging his feet, refusing to act despite the threat to his future, had Paul made a move?

"What would Paul have to gain from stealing a script?" I asked Marion.

"The same thing Ethan wants, I guess," Marion said shakily. "Fame. It *is* a good concept. A really good one, in fact."

"Would Paul have any reason to blackmail or coerce you into taking on the project with him in some capacity?"

Marion's expression darkened. "I haven't slept with

Paul."

"That's not what I mean."

Marion reached up and tugged at his hair. "I think John told me, even though he was drunk, because he wants me to seriously consider the script. Projects I want get well funded. They get noticed. I'm not being egotistical. That's the truth. I know that's Ethan's plan, at least—if he can rip that idea out from underneath John's feet—to ride my coattails to the top." He motioned with his hand. "Maybe Paul would do the same."

I stood, took Marion's hand, and hauled him to his feet. I reached into my pocket and handed him my tin of Altoids. "Here."

He smiled a little, almost like that simple gesture was going to undo him. "Thanks." He tapped a few mints out and popped them into his mouth.

"Come with me." I took his hand and led him out of the dressing room.

"Where are—Rory, where are we going now?"

"If Paul's overheard our conversation, he's going to pack up and hightail it out of here." I led the way through staging and toward the far corner where crew kept their belongings in assigned lockers. "I need some kind of tangible evidence that proves Paul stole the script, if not the script itself among his belongings."

"He wouldn't be stupid enough to keep it *here*, would he?" Marion asked, now willingly following instead of trying to pull away. His hand changed grip, moved to thread his fingers between mine.

"Sometimes hiding a hot item in plain sight is the smartest thing to do," I murmured as we passed the art department and kept walking.

Marion came to a halt outside the lockers. He was frowning deeply. "How would the evidence be viable if you obtained it without permission?"

"These aren't secured," I said, glancing at Marion briefly. "The lockers don't belong to any one individual. And John gave me all the permission I need." I popped open the first one and took a peek inside.

"I don't know which one is Paul's," Marion said. He crouched to check the lower level. "But he wears a green ski coat."

"That's good," I answered, moving from door to door as quickly as possible.

Marion opened another locker and swore as a pile of loose paperwork spilled out across the floor. He scrambled to collect all the sheets, then audibly gasped.

"What is it?" I bent down beside him.

Marion nodded his chin at the locker. "This is Ethan's. I'd know that stupid leather jacket anywhere. But look at this." He sifted through what were clearly disorganized script pages, before he found the title cover. "*Sunrise*," he read. "By… hold on… Davey Heller?" Marion looked at me. "Why would Ethan have a script written by *Davey*?"

The broken photocopier.

Building construction—tarps and buckets.

A vacant and unlit hallway.

Drywall dust.

"Davey was making copies of his script," I said in a drawn-out, almost thoughtful tone. "But he used the copier in the vacant office space to hide the fact that he was using supplies for personal gain. Ethan saw him carrying this." I took the stack of loose paper from Marion and held it up. "A script. And Davey's acting squirrely. Ethan suspects Davey has somehow found out about John's script and is trying to sneak off with it. He surprises Davey in the empty hall, tries to forcefully take it. Davey fights him, protective of his own intellectual property. There was a struggle, and it escalated."

Marion's mismatched eyes were wide with horror and grief. "But—"

"Ethan had something on his pant leg yesterday morning. I didn't think much of it." I handed Marion back the papers. "But if he'd been crouched behind Davey, a knee on the floor as he wrapped a cord around his neck…." I demonstrated. "His pant leg would pick up what was on the floor."

"And what was that?"

"White dust—*drywall* dust. From the construction. Ethan must have run with the script, but by the time he got to staging, realized *this* script had nothing to do with John. He hid it in his locker, then went to your dressing room while I was with you."

Marion looked down at the crumpled pages, absently smoothing down creases. "Poor Davey…. Now what?"

INT. CHAPTER TEN - DAY

Working until lunch break had been… troubling. Marion hadn't wanted to return to set, not after the likely truth of his murderous ex-boyfriend had come to light in the spilled pages of a script never destined for the camera. And I couldn't blame him. I didn't want Marion within a hundred feet of that rat bastard Ethan. I didn't want *anyone* around Ethan.

But I couldn't make my move yet. The minute I phoned Grey, my cover would be blown. I had nothing on Paul but Marion's sureness that the sound recordist had been listening in on private conversations. And only wishy-washy, circumstantial evidence against Ethan, which might be *just* enough for Grey to receive a search warrant for the dust-coated jeans of yesterday. So if I was going to call the police to back me up after having reached the limits of my investigative license, I'd be damned if I'd settle for anything less than Ethan in handcuffs and Paul at John's mercy.

"Rory!"

I came to an abrupt stop outside the big open door leading to the set. I looked over my shoulder and felt myself relax as Marion rushed across staging. His costume shoes *tap, tap tapp*ed the entire way. "Go back to lunch," I insisted. "Safety in numbers."

"Says the man wandering around production alone." Marion came to a stop beside me. "What are you doing?"

"I need to scope out the set for more evidence. There's a lot of equipment right in the open."

Marion blinked a few times as he caught on. "But because union guidelines don't allow departments to touch one another's gear... hiding in plain sight."

"Right."

"I'll help."

I quickly put a hand on his chest to stop him. "We can't allow Paul to see us both absent. It's too obvious."

"I rarely stay for the entire meal," he answered.

I moved my hand up and cupped Marion's jaw. "I've been doing this since you were in junior high. Trust me." I kissed his mouth lightly and took a step through the doorway.

I heard Marion let out a held breath and say after me, "Has anyone told you how fine you look for your age?"

A grin crossed my face, but I didn't look back.

I heard his footsteps retreat after a moment, and I was left completely alone on the dimly lit, silent set. I carefully moved around light stands, piles of sandbags, and wrangled cables as I moved deeper into the room. Paul's sound cart was where it had been all week. There were no drawers, merely shelves housing a state-of-the-art mixing board and a few recording devices. The bottom part had a plethora of cases, small leather satchels I'd seen him pull various tools of the trade from—moleskin, Topstick, nail scissors, even a box of unlubricated condoms, the latter being something I'd not yet learned the importance of while on a film set. But they weren't big enough to stuff a thick stack of paper into.

Another bag of suitable size was empty but for a few pairs of unused headphones. I stood, rubbed my lightly bristled chin, then turned on one heel. The hard shell equipment boxes were still stacked against the far wall. Stickers of competing companies adorned the outsides, fighting for limited advertising space. They were Paul's. I'd first seen him go into one the day he needed a cable made. I walked forward, unsnapped the top case, and looked inside.

Nothing.

I closed the lid, pushed it aside, and crouched to open a bigger one. There was some kind of mixer-looking gadget safely tucked into the foam specially shaped for the gear. I started to close the box as the convoluted foam fell. I muttered a swear and pushed it back into the top of the lid, then paused to stare at it.

Removable.

I leaned the lid against the wall, carefully took out the equipment, then hoisted out the middle section of foam. Underneath was a stack of white printer paper, held together by a binder clip. I picked it up, angled it toward a nearby security light, and read, *John Anderson*, across the title page.

I let out a quiet *whoosh* of air. All right. I'd have to put this back. Assemble everything just the way I found it, and give my evidence against Paul to John. The producer would have the authority to search—

"Son of a bitch!"

I was hit in the face and went sprawling sideways across the floor, script tossed somewhere in the dark. My tortoiseshell glasses dug into the side of my nose and snapped in two, leaving me at a distinct disadvantage. I slowly raised myself up on one arm and spit blood from my mouth.

"Who the fuck are you?"

I turned my neck with considerable difficulty, to see Ethan holding one of those foldable, high-legged director's seats. The asshole had hit me with a goddamn chair. "Rory Byrne," I answered.

"I don't care what your name is," he said. "I asked who you *were*. A cop?"

"No."

"You're sure as shit not a PA."

"No," I said before spitting again.

"*No,*" he agreed. "Because a PA would never be so stupid as to suck face with Marion Roosevelt out in the open for anyone to see." He walked toward me, holding the collapsed chair like he was ready to beat my ass with it. "Do you have any idea who *I* am, Rory Byrne?"

"I know exactly who you are. A murderer."

That gave Ethan pause. He wasn't expecting that sort of response. Wasn't expecting some nobody to be aware of his crime.

It was enough for me to scramble to my feet and lunge for the script. But the chair came down on my back with a deafening *smash*, and I collapsed. The wind was knocked from my lungs, and I gasped like a fish out of water. I tilted my head where I lay, watched Ethan toss the mangled furniture to the floor, and walk to the script.

He bent down, retrieved it, and stared at the title page for a moment. "How did you find this?" Ethan looked at me.

I winced, managed to swallow a shallow breath of air, and started to get up on my knees, when a suppressed shot rang out from behind me. Ethan screamed as he crumpled to the floor. It happened so quickly, I literally couldn't react accordingly.

Not to my own pain.

Not to the sound of a gun using an illegal silencer.

Or the fact that Ethan had just been shot.

My adrenaline went into overdrive, and I scrambled the rest of the way to my knees.

"Don't move," Paul ordered, his voice too close for comfort.

I froze, hands up in surrender. "Paul," I said, my voice almost steady. "I'm unarmed."

"I know."

I dared a quick look toward Ethan. He was alive, curled in the fetal position, and whimpering. The script had fallen nearby and was soaked in blood. "Can I stand?"

"No," Paul answered without hesitation. "You move, and I swear to God, I'll pull the trigger."

"All right," I said slowly. "But listen, we need to get help for Ethan—"

"*Shut. Up,*" Paul hissed.

I struggled for a plan, but I'd been dealt a dud hand in this round of poker. We were alone. My phone was in my pocket. Ethan was of no help. Paul was in fight-or-flight mode. And while silencers didn't work like movies portrayed them, no way would folks all the way in the lunch room have heard the *pop*.

All I had on my side was a bluff.

"Paul," I said again, keeping my voice low so as not to startle him.

"*What?*" he snapped. The rubber of his sneakers squeaked against the floor as he moved to the equipment cases and closed the lids.

"I have backup coming."

"I heard you," Paul answered in between the snapping of the locks. "You aren't a cop."

"No, you're right, I'm not." Sweat prickled under my arms. "I'm a private investigator."

"Who'd you call, then?"

"Detective Grey," I lied. "He's a homicide detective with the 105th Precinct. He was here yesterday when I found Davey."

"Let him come," Paul answered. He moved past, gun trained on me with one shaking hand as he bent to retrieve the script. "If Ethan killed Davey, he deserves to rot in a cell."

I watched Paul's blurry shape walk to my right and then disappear from my line of sight as he moved behind me again. "And what do you deserve if you shoot me?"

Paul didn't have an answer to that.

"You can't use John's script as your own. You can't even take the idea now. You've been caught."

"I said shut the hell up," Paul warned again. "*Damn it.* If you'd just kept your fucking nose out of it, Rory—"

"I couldn't do that."

"No, of course not," he spat. "I knew you'd come here to sniff around after I heard you talking with Marion." Paul laughed, full of vitriol. "That overpaid prima-donna actor living off the laurels of us nobodies instead of accepting he's a commodity—"

Paul was interrupted by a sudden scream. There

was a *thwack*, a *crack*, and then the unmistakable sound of a pistol sliding across the floor. I jumped to my feet and turned to see Marion's outline in the poor lighting. He was breathing hard, visibly shaking, and holding a graphite boom pole in his hands like a bat. Paul had crumpled to the floor like a ragdoll after a knock to the back of the head.

"He—he was going to *shoot you*," Marion protested.

I nodded in agreement as I reached for the fallen weapon. I got down on one knee beside Paul, put two fingers to his neck, and felt his pulse. "He's alive. Going to have a hell of a headache when he comes around, though." I went to Marion, pried the pole out of his hands, and took him into my arms. "Thanks," I whispered as he wrapped himself tight around me.

EXT. CHAPTER ELEVEN – DAY

I stood outside of Kaufman Astoria Studios with a few dozen other cast and crew members of *The Bowery*, watching the ambulance crews pack up Ethan and Paul into their own buses.

"You sure you want to refuse medical treatment?" Grey asked.

I briefly removed the ice pack from my jaw. "I've still got all my teeth."

"He hit you with a chair."

Like I needed to be reminded.

"Paul will be okay, right?" Marion asked. He'd been all but glued to my side since we'd phoned 911 and effectively shut down another day of production. "I *had* to hit him," he insisted for probably the dozenth time.

"He was going to shoot Rory."

Grey held up a hand. "He's going to be fine, Mr. Roosevelt. Had you not acted, Byrne might have ended up with more than simply a bruised jaw."

"You saved Rory's life," John agreed as he turned away from the ambulances. "But why were you even on set, honey?"

"That's a good question," I said while looking down at Marion. "Not that I'm upset, but I'm pretty certain I told you to *go away*."

"I did," Marion answered. "I'd barely reached crafty when Ethan stopped me. He saw you kiss me before going on set."

Grey gave me a you-dog look.

I ignored it.

Marion swallowed, pinched the bridge of his nose, and shook his head. "We've been broken up for six months, but he's so… he still tries to control what I do. Who I see. He said he was going to beat the shit out of you."

"He did a fairly decent job," I remarked.

"Because I was afraid to stop him," Marion murmured, finally looking up. "But he's—a *killer*. I couldn't leave you alone with him."

I put an arm around Marion's slender shoulders and gave him a sideways hug.

"And when you went after Mr. Lefkowitz?" Grey pressed.

"Paul was already in there," Marion answered. "Maybe he'd been in there the entire time, or came through the side entrance, I don't know. But I saw the gun—saw Rory with his hands up—so I grabbed the first thing I could find. When I was pretty certain I had a half-second's chance of stopping him…." Marion motioned swinging a bat.

The ambulances turned their sirens on and pulled out of the studio driveway.

Grey motioned John aside to speak semi-privately.

I dropped my arm from Marion's shoulders and pressed the ice pack to my jaw again. "I'm sorry."

He moved to stand in front of me. "For?"

"For my accusations earlier."

Marion squinted a little as the sun peeked out from behind winter clouds. "Did you really believe I'd lied to you? That I could have stolen the script?"

I considered the question for a long while. Cold air puffed around my face as I breathed. "No… but… I'm a rational, work-obsessed person. I follow the rules. *The facts.*"

"And the facts were stacked against me?"

"I felt like I *had* to believe them. Even though I didn't want to." I lowered the ice pack. "I wasn't joking, Marion. I'm no good at the stuff that happens afterward. That's why I have an extensive ex-boyfriends list."

He chewed his lower lip for a moment as he stared at the road. "Maybe you need more rehearsals."

"Come again?"

Marion looked up, and his mouth quirked into that smile I loved so much. "And if we need to go off script to figure it out, that's fine. It doesn't matter."

"I thought movie-making required teamwork."

"Two makes a team." He took the ice pack from my hand and gently pressed it to my face. "The MET is having a special exhibit on Kuniyoshi and his woodblock art of cats. There's a really great Indian restaurant nearby too. If you're free later."

My jaw was throbbing, but it didn't stop the smile from breaking out across my face.

FADE OUT

Rory Byrne and Marion Roosevelt return in:

Action on Murder.
(The Silver Screen: Case Two)

C.S. Poe is a Lambda Literary and two-time EPIC award finalist, and a FAPA award-winning author of gay mystery, romance, and speculative fiction.

She resides in New York City, but has also called Key West and Ibaraki, Japan, home in the past. She has an affinity for all things cute and colorful and a major weakness for toys. C.S. is an avid fan of coffee, reading, and cats. She's rescued two cats—Milo and Kasper do their best to distract her from work on a daily basis.

C.S. is an alumna of the School of Visual Arts.

Her debut novel, *The Mystery of Nevermore*, was published 2016.

cspoe.com

ALSO BY C.S. POE

SERIES:

Snow & Winter

The Mystery of Nevermore

The Mystery of the Curiosities

The Mystery of the Moving Image

The Mystery of the Bones

Magic & Steam

The Engineer

A Lancaster Story

Kneading You

Joy

Color of You

The Silver Screen

Lights. Camera. Murder.

NOVELS:

Southernmost Murder

NOVELLAS:

11:59

SHORT STORIES:
Love in 24 Frames
That Turtle Story
New Game, Start
Love, Marriage, and a Baby Carriage
Love Has No Expiration

Visit **cspoe.com** for free slice-of-life codas, titles in audio, and available foreign translations.

Join C.S. Poe's mailing list to stay updated on upcoming releases, sales, conventions, and more!
bit.ly/CSPocNewsletter